I0629770

Scottish Knight

The Young Explorers, Volume 3

S T Cameron

Published by S T Cameron, 2025.

While every precaution has been taken in the preparation of this book, the publisher assumes no responsibility for errors or omissions, or for damages resulting from the use of the information contained herein.

SCOTTISH KNIGHT

First edition. July 17, 2025.

Copyright © 2025 S T Cameron.

ISBN: 979-8886230390

Written by S T Cameron.

To Chloe, Julian, Mae, and Jarrett

For whom I wrote this story

Chapter 1

Oorlich, Scotland 1537

The pouring rain and booming thunder of the storm raging outside the small, thatched cottage meant nothing to the old woman. Neither did the screams of the infant inside the cottage as she moved about, gathering the ingredients she would need. The infant's mother clutched the swaddled girl to her chest, trying to will the baby's cries to stop, but the screams continued as they had since the night before. Her husband held his wife with one arm and pressed his other hand on the bundled girl's back. He glanced at the old woman as she brewed the elixir.

"You are sure that it will cure her?" he asked, but the woman just mumbled to herself as she added ingredient after ingredient to the potion warming over the fire.

The husband stole a glance at his wife.

One of their neighbors told them she had cured her young son of a pox that had turned the boy's tongue black. Everyone whispered among themselves that she was a witch and the mother refused to visit her at first. But when the little girl's cries became screams, they came calling at the woman's door.

"Hestor..." the man began.

"Shush!" the woman cut him off. Taking the cup with the elixir off of the flames, she set it on the table to cool. She grabbed a small brown bottle from a shelf crowded with a multitude of other bottles and placed it beside the cup.

She turned to the mother and reached for the baby.

"I'm not sure I..." the man tried to say as he stepped between the witch and his daughter.

"Do you want her to die?" The woman scowled up at him. Another peal of thunder seemed to emphasize her mood. Her eyes, sunk deep in the ruts of her wrinkles, reflected the light from the fire, giving her a more menacing appearance than her small stature normally would.

The man moved his mouth, but the words wouldn't come.

Hestor pushed him aside and grabbed the screaming infant. The mother's hold on the child gave way along with her resistance to the witch.

The woman laid the baby gently on the table next to the potion.

She picked up the brown bottle and placed three drops into the cup with the rest of the liquid.

The man recognized a symbol on the bottle's label.

"That's a poison!" The man tried to grab the child away from the old woman.

The woman held the child on the table. "Only in large quantities," she told him. "Now stand back and let me save this child."

The man shrank back next to his wife. He grasped her hands as she mumbled a prayer.

The woman mixed the potion once again. Using her finger, she dripped the liquid into the screaming child's open mouth. The screams stopped as the girl began choking on the elixir.

The couple started forward, but the old woman's hand stopped them in their tracks.

"She'll be fine," she said. "Let me do this." She continued dripping the liquid into the baby's mouth.

The screams and coughs died down as the girl swallowed the potion as fast as the old woman could drip it into her mouth.

Suddenly, the sound of horses galloping through the wet roads up to the front of the cottage replaced the sound of the girl's screams.

A sharp knocking startled the couple, but the woman ignored it and continued to feed the potion to the infant.

There was another sharp knock, followed by a shout.

"Open this door by the order of Lord MacGregor!" a man shouted from outside.

The couple looked at each other with fear. The old woman did not respond to the order.

There was a crack. The door broke open and two of the Lord's guards, dripping with the storm's deluge, lunged into the cottage.

"You there," one guard yelled at Hestor. "Stop that!"

The two guards grabbed the arms of the woman, who put down the cup before they overpowered her.

"You are under arrest for murder and practicing witchcraft. You will come with us and stand before the Lord this very night," the guard told her. Two other guards appeared at the door to help.

"I must give this medicine to that child," the woman protested. "Else, it will die."

"You've already killed another child!" the guard shouted. "We won't allow you to kill another."

The guards at the door backed out of the cottage as the other two dragged the old woman out into the mud of the street.

"Feed her the rest," Hestor yelled to the couple over the din of the storm. "Finish it if you want her to live."

The guards bound her by chains to the cart waiting outside and mounted their horses. At once, they started off down the road, pulling the woman stumbling through the mud after them.

The couple shivered in the wind that swept into the broken cottage and looked at each other, both white as sheets.

The mother quickly bundled their daughter up and gathered her into her arms. She went to the door and looked out at the storm pouring rain across the village and countryside. She looked back at her husband, who hadn't moved.

He looked at his wife with wide eyes. When she nodded out at the storm, he turned, grabbed the cup with the remaining elixir, and joined her in the doorway.

Then they both slipped out into the storm. The man held his hand over the top of the cup to protect the potion until they could get home and give the rest to their little girl.

Chapter 2

The stench in the dungeon cell below Castle MacGregor was a mixture of vomit, excrement, and rotting straw. When they threw a prisoner into the cell, it often made them sick enough to add their own contribution to the smell. But after a few hours, they no longer noticed anything but a massive pain in their head.

They imprisoned Hestor long enough that she no longer noticed it. She sat on the floor next to the gate, whispering with her daughter and young granddaughter. They were not yet immune to the odors.

"What are they going to do with you?" her daughter asked.

"I'm accused of being a witch," Hestor said. "What do you think they're going to do?"

Her granddaughter hid her face in her hands and sobbed.

"Now, Eisla," Hestor said, reaching through the bars and stroking the young girl's long black hair. "Everything will be fine."

"Don't lie to her," her daughter said. "It will not be fine."

"Kellina. You and Eisla will be fine."

"What about you? He won't let you go this time."

"Maybe not. But, I've done what I can in this life. And it's been a long one."

"Are you just giving up?" Kellina asked.

"No," Hestor said. "I will do what I can to appease..." She paused and looked away into the darkness of the cell. "... or fight back."

"What are you planning?"

Hestor turned back to Kellina and smiled. "Nothing you need to worry about."

"Can we ask Lord MacGregor to let Gramma go?" Eisla asked the two.

"I'm going to," Kellina said.

The door to the dungeon opened with a screech and a clunk, startling the young girl. She moved closer to her mother, and they held each other as the guards came to the cell door.

"The Lord requires your presence," one guard told Hestor as she rose to her feet and shook the straw from her dress.

"Let's not disappoint him," Hestor said. "Lead the way."

The guards led the woman out of the dungeon, with Kellina and Eisla following behind.

They brought Hestor before Lord MacGregor in the great hall he used for formal meetings and, as on this night, trials. He sat on a heavy wooden throne behind a long table on a dais three steps up from the main floor. A smaller chair flanked the throne on both sides. The one to his right was empty, but his eleven-year-old son, Euan, occupied the one to his left.

They brought Hestor to the bottom of the steps and pushed her down on her knees in front of the table. The guards stopped Kellina and Eisla in the back of the hall.

"Welcome to Castle MacGregor," the Lord said, laughing.

"Thank you, M'Lord," Hestor said. She kept her voice low.

"Do you know why you are here?"

"Many reasons, I'm sure."

"They have accused you of being a witch and a murderer."

"Is that the real reason?" Hestor asked.

Lord MacGregor narrowed his eyes at the old woman. "What other reason could I have?"

"You may still harbor bitterness that I wasn't able to save M'Lady after she gave birth to your son."

The Lord glanced at the boy, who sat staring at the floor. He glared back at Hestor. "Don't mention my wife again!"

"I am sorry, M'Lord," Hestor said, bowing forward. "Am I wrong?"

Lord MacGregor didn't reply. He looked up at the guard at the back of the hall.

"Bring in the witness," he commanded.

Several guards pushed the two-story doors open and gestured to a red-haired woman waiting outside. She entered and approached the dais, stopping a few feet to the right of the old woman.

"What is your name, child?" the Lord asked her gently.

"Marjary, M'Lord."

Hestor could see several bruises on Marjary's face and hands, along with the redness of rope burns around her wrists.

Marjary remained silent for several minutes. She glanced down at Hestor, tears in her eyes.

"Don't worry, dear. Tell them what you need to." Hestor told her quietly.

Marjary closed her eyes and looked up at Lord MacGregor.

"The witch... Hestor..." she began. Her body shook, and she swallowed hard. "She made a potion she said would cure my little Brodie."

"And did it?" the Lord asked.

Marjory held her hands up to her eyes and wiped her tears.

"No," she said, barely audibly.

"There we have it. Your witchcraft murdered her son." Lord MacGregor boomed.

"He was too far gone," Hestor told the woman. "I tried my best, but it wasn't enough."

"I know," the woman whispered.

"You tried your best to kill him," the Lord said. "And you succeeded."

"No!" Kellina shouted from the back. "She always tries to help people."

The Lord stood and shouted, "Quiet!" Then he pointed at her and commanded the guards to bring her forward.

The guards escorted her roughly before the dais. Another guard grabbed Eisla and dragged her to the front as well.

"Who are you?" He demanded.

"I am her daughter, Kellina," she told him.

"Why should I take your word that she isn't a witch?"

Hestor shook her head at Kellina.

"Ask anyone. She's helped many people in the village who were sick or ailing."

"I did. I asked this woman," he said, waving his hand toward Marjary.

"Ask other people." Kellina insisted. "It's not possible to save everyone."

"She refused to save my wife," The Lord asked.

"She didn't refuse. She couldn't save her. But there are many others she has helped." She said.

The Lord sat back in his chair and touched his lip with his finger. After several minutes, he leaned forward again and waved his hand at the guards.

"Stand for the verdict," one guard said, and pulled Hestor to her feet.

"After some deliberation, I find you... not guilty of murder," the Lord said with a smile.

Kellina, Eisla, and Marjory breathed audible sighs of relief.

Hestor simply stared at Lord MacGregor, seemingly not breathing at all.

The smile disappeared from the Lord's face as he stood.

"However, I find you guilty of being a witch," he said in a low tone. "Your house will be burned to the ground along with all of the the evil things inside."

"No!" Kellina shouted.

MacGregor continued "You will be taken from here to the courtyard of the castle, where I will behead you myself. May God have mercy on your soul."

After glaring at her a moment longer, the Lord turned and left the hall. Kellina collapsed to the floor.

The guards took hold of the old woman and escorted her out of the hall, a look of determination darkening her face.

Chapter 3

The news of the coming execution spread quickly throughout the village. Despite the receding storm and the darkness, villagers filed through the gates and filled the edges of the courtyard. They talked in excited whispers at first, but the conversations gained in volume as the space filled with other noisy villagers.

Before the guards could place the basket in front of the block on the raised platform in the center of the castle's courtyard, a crowd filled the surrounding space. Some in the crowd were gawkers who wanted to see the witch die. Others were there to witness the passing of the woman they sympathized with.

Moving among the crowd were people with other motives for being there. Jugglers, minstrels, and other street performers milled through the crowd with their songs and entertainment, looking for appreciative patrons to throw a few coins in their hat.

Merchants set up carts to sell fragrant pies, strong ale, and execution memorabilia to the people massed in the yard, not able to get away. For many of them, it would be their best sales in many days.

The courtyard had a carnival-like atmosphere with an abundance of laughing, feasting, and singing. An atmosphere far from the serious nature of what was about to occur.

The doors to the keep opened to reveal four guards who escorted the old woman out into the courtyard. The doors closed again behind them.

At first, the crowd focused on the party and didn't notice. Soon, people started falling silent and elbowing others who hadn't seen the entrance of the witch.

After a few moments of quiet, hecklers started taunting her.

"Oh, my. Look who's gonna die," one man shouted.

"You'll see Satan in hell tonight," another one said, waving a tattered Bible in the air.

Then the crowd began laughing and cheering all over again.

One man threw an egg at the old woman, but it missed her and splattered against the boots of one guard. He grabbed his sword and pulled it a few inches out of his scabbard, glaring in the direction where the egg came from. There were no more eggs thrown that night.

He let the sword slide back down into the scabbard and turned to help his fellow guards hoist the old woman up onto the platform.

Once at the top, her hands were bound behind her, and they forced her to kneel before the block. They pulled the top of her robe down, exposing her neck and shoulders.

The guards stepped back and stood at attention in a circle around the woman so that she could not attempt to escape her fate.

When all was ready, they stood silent. The crowd hushed in anticipation of the coming spectacle.

The doors to the keep opened once more and Lord MacGregor strode out into the courtyard, followed by his young son, Euan.

Lord MacGregor wore his full plate armor. His long sword was in a scabbard tied around his waist, and he tucked his helmet under one arm. He moved smoothly and easily in the armor up to the platform and looked around the courtyard, waving his arm in greeting. The armor gleamed in the torch light of the courtyard.

Euan wore a smaller set of plate mail. He had no helmet or sword. He tripped as he climbed the steps to the platform.

Coughs and snorts erupted throughout the crowd as they tried to stifle their laughs at the boy. Lord MacGregor scowled at them until the noise died down again.

After he righted himself, the boy stood quietly behind his father. His face was beet red.

"This woman is guilty of witchcraft and is sentenced to die," the Lord said over the low din of the crowd.

A few 'Kill the witch!' shouts came from several places in the courtyard.

Lord MacGregor smiled and continued, "We must root out these witches from wherever they hide in the land. They must not gain a foothold in our village or turn us against one another."

More people in the crowd shouted in agreement.

"Tonight, we will rid ourselves of this one, but we must be vigilant and root out any others that we can find," he said and looked at Hestor's daughter and granddaughter, who stood by the doors to the keep.

"Kill the witch!" The chant began throughout the crowd and grew until most of them joined in. Lord MacGregor smiled and let them go on for several minutes.

Then he motioned for quiet.

"But I am not eager for blood," he said. "If the witch will renounce Satan and give up her evil ways, it might persuade me to simply banish her from this place."

He turned to Hestor and smiled down at her.

"Will you give up your witchcraft and lead a more pious life away from here?" He asked her.

He waited for her answer. The crowd grew silent as they too waited to see if she would agree.

"All that I can promise you is..." Hestor began. And then she started to chant.

"Darkness will fall, and light will flee.
Alone, without shield and guard, you'll be."

"Silence her," the Lord shouted to his guards.

"Evil you wrought, and evil you spread,
All bringing a curse down onto your head."

The guards grabbed her arms, and one covered her mouth with his hand. He screamed and pulled his hand away to find blood gushing from the gash she bit into it.

She spit out a bit of his flesh and continued.

"As now you cut and as you rend,
Thus, will all the Lords here end."

A flash of lightning lit up the courtyard and a peal of thunder rolled over the village. The crowd gasped and fell back away from the platform where the old woman kneeled, laughing.

"Place her on the block," Lord MacGregor said.

The guards pulled her forward and laid her head on the bloody block.

The Lord stepped forward and pulled out his sword and raised it over his head.

Kellina pulled Eisla to her and forced her to look away.

The sword was swift and true. Blood splattered against the block, the guards, and the platform. The witch was dead.

Chapter 4

Lord MacGregor stormed into the antechamber of his private quarters. Several maids were waiting for him with rags to wipe the blood from his armor.

"Damn witch," he snapped.

He noticed the maids sneaking glances behind him. He turned to find his son standing at the door, still in his armor, blood splattered on the armor and on his face.

"What are you doing there?" he yelled at him. "Get cleaned up." Tears ran down the boy's face.

"I will assist Master Euan," one maid said, rushing to help him out the door and to his own quarters.

"Wait!" the man told her.

He turned to his son. "As the master of this castle, I have many responsibilities. And that includes keeping order and punishing those that break our laws. Do you understand?"

The boy nodded and wiped the tears and blood from his face.

"When it is your time to be Lord of this castle, you will have to be brave enough to do the same," he said, "and you can't be crying about it all the time."

Euan sniffed once and stood in silence before his father.

"Go now and get out of that armor," he told the boy. The boy turned and fled the room with the maid after him.

"I hope he'll be ready when it is his time," the Lord said quietly to himself.

The other two maids helped him remove his armor, clean the pieces, and reassemble them on the stand in a tall cabinet. The sword hung from a hook beside it as the cabinet was closed.

Once the Lord cleaned up and dressed for bed, he dismissed the maids.

He sat at a small table where they left a few morsels for him to eat before he retired to the bedroom. He finished the bread, cold venison, and warm ale and leaned back in his chair to review the events of the day.

The muffled sound of metal against metal rang out from behind him. He jumped up and spun around. But there was nothing to see. No one was there.

The cabinet door slowly creaked open. As he approached it, the door suddenly opened wide. The sword tipped out and clattered onto the floor.

He breathed a sigh of relief. "Will they ever learn to put things away securely?" he asked himself. He picked the sword up, threw open the cabinet door, and hung it back on the hook.

"Probably not." He slammed the cabinet door shut, blew out the candles in the antechamber and went into the bedroom for the night.

The bed took up most of the room, with a towering wooden post at each corner carved like a yew tree, with gnarled branches coming together to form a canopy over the bed.

He turned the key in the bedroom door and listened for any more noises emanating from the antechamber, but it was as silent as the grave.

"Damn witch," he said again. "She's got me on edge."

He extinguished the candles about the room, leaving the bedroom in shadows except for the light of the low fire that burned in the massive stone fireplace.

He crawled under the covers and settled down for the night. After a few additional moments of listening for sounds, he hunkered down under the covers and tried to sleep.

Hours later, he awoke to a banging. He sat up and scanned the room.

Everything was as it had been and as it should be. He listened, but heard nothing more.

Did he hear something, or was it part of a dream? He wasn't sure.

He lay back on the bed again when suddenly, there was a thunderous bang on the bedroom door. He jumped out of bed and stood before the door, listening.

"Who's there?" he demanded.

Something thudded against the door again. He could see the door vibrate.

"Guards!" he yelled. "Come at once!"

Another thud. The door buckled.

"Guards!" he screamed louder. "Where are you?"

The next thud caused the door to splinter open toward him. He fell back away from it and grabbed an iron poker from the stand next to the fireplace and held it up in front of him like a sword.

In the doorway was a man in armor wielding an actual sword. But when he looked again, he realized the intruder was wearing not just any armor, but his own armor and he was using his sword.

The intruder closed the distance and swung at the Lord. The weapon clanged against the poker and glanced away.

"Guards!" the Lord called again. "I need you!"

The intruder was relentless and swung the sword at the Lord again and again. The Lord could defend himself with the poker, but he knew it was just a matter of time before it would overpower him.

"Who are you?" the Lord yelled at the intruder.

The intruder raised his sword over his head. As the Lord prepared the poker to meet the attack, he saw it.

He could see into the helmet of the knight because the faceplate was up. There was no face inside, no face and no head.

"What are you?" he screamed.

When the sword came down against the poker again, it knocked the Lord backward on the floor. The poker skidded away under the bed.

The Lord pushed himself back away from the intruder, who strode forward to him.

The sword flashed one more time, and then it was still.

Euan ran to his father's bedroom when he heard the cry of the guards. The maid who tended to him earlier in the evening tried to prevent him from entering the room, but he got around her and saw the bloody scene.

His father lay on the floor with his suit of armor standing over him. The hands of the knight clamped on the sword hilt, with the blade balanced on the floor at the spot where his father's head should have been. It did not move.

"Witchcraft," he said.

He glanced around at the guards and the maids in the room. They were all looking at him. It took him a moment to realize they were waiting for his orders. His father was dead. It was up to him now to take charge.

"We need to get rid of it," he said. "What can we do with it?"

"Drop it to the bottom of the lake," one guard suggested.

"It's just armor. It won't drown," the boy replied. He moved up closer to the armor and peered at it.

"Careful there," another guard said.

"What about rocks?" someone suggested.

"Rocks won't break it unless they are huge rocks," another said.

"What about the east garden?" Euan said. "Father was having part of it paved with heavy stone blocks. Maybe we can bury it with stone blocks on top."

"Can we get it down there?" a guard asked.

"See if it will let you carry it," the boy said.

The guards tentatively approached the suit of armor. They placed their hands on it and lifted it while another guard attempted to take the sword from it.

The armor did not resist. In a matter of a few hours, they buried it in the east garden with a dozen heavy stone blocks stacked on top of it.

Only then did everyone breathe again.

Chapter 5

Scotland, June 1919

C.J. Kask was on the viewing deck of the Falcon II, a state-of-the-art airship that had been his home for the last week as he flew from Minnesota, over New York City, and across the Atlantic Ocean to Ireland. Now they were approaching Scotland and their destination, MacGregor Castle in Oorlich.

C.J., at only thirteen-years-old, was already a veteran of several archaeological expeditions at places all around the world. But this next one seemed more like it was going to be a vacation.

With him were Sadie and Scotty MacGregor, two of his fellow Young Explorers and relatives of Alastair MacGregor, the current Lord MacGregor.

Lord MacGregor was having part of the castle excavated prior to building a new wing and invited Sadie and Scotty's father, Walter, his cousin, to come visit and take part in the excavation.

"Are you excited to see your family's castle?" C.J. asked Sadie.

"It's their castle, not ours. We're just related to them," she told him.

Sadie was the same age as C.J. and was just as excited about archaeology as him.

"I can't wait to see the castle." Scotty piped up. "I love the architecture."

Scotty was two years younger than his sister and seemed to be an expert on everything having to do with architecture and engineering.

"Are we almost there?" a girl's voice said behind them. Laura Hall, another member of their Young Explorers group, joined them on the viewing deck. She was carrying her Gaelic language textbook. They spoke Gaelic in Scotland and the twelve-year-old was trying to learn as much as she could before they arrived. She loved learning languages as much as Scotty loved building things.

"No sign of Scotland yet," Sadie told her. "Soon though, I hope."

Edna MacGregor appeared at the door to the viewing deck.

"Time for lunch," she said. "Come across to the dining salon."

The four headed out for the lunch after one last quick look down at the waves below them.

Their parents were already seated at the table when they got to the dining salon.

"What have you kids been up to?" Angus Kask asked.

"Just watching for Scotland." C.J. told his father.

"We'll get there soon," Walter MacGregor said.

"We're just excited to see the castle," Scotty said. His mother and father nodded.

"We know," Edna said, "it's all you've talked about since we left home."

"An urrainn dhut Gàidhlig a bhruidhinn?" Teresa Hall asked her daughter.

"Tha mi air cuid ionnsachadh," Laura said.

"What was that?" C.J. asked.

"I asked Laura if she could speak Gaelic."

"And I told her I've learned some."

Both Jackson and Teresa Hall smiled at their daughter.

A server appeared from the kitchen on the deck below with a platter full of sandwiches. Another server brought cold water and iced tea.

C.J. didn't realize until that moment how hungry he was. He glanced around and saw the other kids scarfing down their food as well.

When everyone was done, Angus dismissed the kids.

"We'll reach the castle in an hour. Change into something more appropriate for meeting a Lord." he said.

The four of them left the dining salon and went to their cabins on the middle deck.

Since there were only eight cabins, C.J. and Scotty shared one.

The cabin was tiny, with just a sink and a small, curtained closet. There was a lower bunk that doubled as a couch during the day. They could lower a second bunk at night. Scotty had claimed the top bunk as soon as they had moved into the cabin.

It wasn't much different from the sleeping cabins on many trains that they had traveled on.

After changing, C.J. visited the lavatories on the lower deck.

The lower desk was where the kitchen was and where the crew had their cabins. It was also where the bathrooms were.

The hatch that opened into the airship itself was also at the bottom of the steps

He was apprehensive at first when he heard they were going to fly on an airship. He had heard that the hydrogen that was used in airships was dangerous and could start on fire and explode.

But this airship used helium, a less dangerous gas. It also meant that the airship had to be small since helium isn't as buoyant as hydrogen. But that was fine with him.

When he returned to the viewing deck, the other three kids were already there.

"Do you see land?" he asked them, leaning over to see through the windows.

"Not yet," Scotty said.

The weather had been good on the Atlantic crossing, but now there was fog ahead of them.

"What do you know about this castle?" Laura asked Sadie.

Sadie lowered her voice. "I've heard it's haunted."

"Really?" C.J. asked.

"Yes," she said, "a banshee shrieks almost every night, signaling someone has died."

"Oh my," Laura gasped.

Scotty giggled.

C.J. scowled at Sadie. "You're just joking around."

Sadie elbowed her brother. "You gave it away."

"I couldn't help it," Scotty said, laughing.

"It's just an old castle," Sadie told them. "No ghosts or banshees. Just some crumbling walls."

"Is it just a ruin?" Laura asked.

"I don't think so." Scotty said. "Lord MacGregor and his family still live in it, so there must be some livable parts."

"Have you ever been there before?" C.J. asked.

"No. We haven't even seen a picture," Sadie told them. "It will be as much of a surprise to us as it will be to you."

"Look!" Laura yelled. The three kids looked in the direction Laura was pointing. Out of the fog ahead of the airship, gray cliffs appeared. They had finally reached the Scottish mainland. They were almost to Scotland and soon after that, Castle MacGregor, the MacGregor Family's ancestral home.

Chapter 6

As the Falcon II sailed over the scenic landscapes of Scotland, the airship's engines, while quieter than a train, startled many of the sheep and cattle that they flew over.

They startled a few people as well. They pointed up to the airship, probably thinking the Great War was back on. Once the kids waved at them from the viewing windows, they usually sheepishly waved back and then returned to whatever it was they were doing.

One boy was riding his bicycle and, when he saw them passing overhead, began pedaling as fast as he could to outrace them. But he soon fell far behind as the road wound through the countryside, but the airship sailed straight through.

They even sailed over a golf course at one point. They were worried that one golfer would drive a ball up into the airship, but soon realized that they were still too high for the golf balls to reach them.

Along the way, they passed over several old castles. Some of them were just ruins, with no one able to live in the rubble. Others were in better shape, with plentiful signs of habitation. They even waved at a woman who held a young child near an open window to wave at them.

Each time, they wondered if that castle was Castle MacGregor, but each time C.J.'s father, who was reading some papers in a high-backed chair, would lean over to see.

"Nope," he would say, and they would go back to watching for it.

The kids felt like they had flown past a hundred castles before Angus' answer changed.

"That's the one," he said finally.

The kids hung over the windows, trying to get a better view of Castle MacGregor. As they got closer, they could see more detail of the castle and the small town surrounding it.

The castle itself was on a hill overlooking the town. They built the keep like a horseshoe wrapped around a central courtyard. Around the keep were massive gardens encircled by walls made of consecutive archways. Over the years, some of those walls broke, scattering stones on the surrounding ground.

On the edge of the hill surrounding the castle was a high wall. At the base of the hill was a moat.

The ditch that was the moat had been wide hundreds of years ago, but now it was just a narrow waterway no bigger than a small stream. They originally designed the wall and the moat to protect the castle from invading armies.

Angus pointed to a wide, flat field just outside the walls.

"The pilot will probably set the ship down there," he told them.

As if in response to his statement, they heard the engines change as they slowed down and circled around the castle toward that open field.

As they flew over the drawbridge that passed over the moat and led through the castle walls, they saw a red-haired girl about their age sitting on the edge of the drawbridge, apparently fishing in the moat.

When she saw them, she jumped up onto the ledge of the drawbridge and frantically waved at them as they passed.

They waved back. As they passed overhead, she jumped down, ran to the other side of the drawbridge and leaped up on the ledge again.

They passed over the town as they descended to their landing. A few people came out to see what the noise of their engines was.

A priest came out and stood on the steps of his church to watch them glide by. He didn't wave.

A young couple was walking in the streets. They looked up and tentatively waved when they saw the kids waving down at them.

An elderly woman with wild white hair stood at the door of her small home with her arms folded in front of her. She just scowled at them and ignored their waves.

A bunch of kids ran out of their school, shouting and waving as they went by. Their teacher ran out of the school after them. She tried in vain to corral them and get them to go back inside.

The airship descended more rapidly as they approached the landing field. The sound of the engines changed once again as they slowed for the final approach.

They had viewed the landing procedures several times before on the trip across the United States and Canada, and this time was no different.

Once they reached a certain altitude, the crew dropped the mooring lines down from the bow and the stern of the craft.

They cranked the exit stairs down. This allowed four of the crew to jump off the ship when it was still several feet off the ground.

Those four would each grab one of the mooring lines and tie it to something that could anchor the airship.

"What are they going to attach the lines to?" Sadie asked Angus.

"They tied us to mooring towers at the airports we stopped at back at home." Scotty said, "They don't have one of those here."

"I'm sure they'll find something," Angus said, "They know what they're doing."

And they found what they needed. The field was not as empty as it first appeared. There were many boulders sunk into its surface, and they could tie the lines securely around them.

"We should head down. We will disembark soon." Angus told them.

They were all standing on the deck below when the airship finally touched down. The crew secured the steps, and the passengers were ready to exit.

One-by-one, they climbed down the stairs and, under the shadow of Castle MacGregor, stepped out into the Scottish countryside. They were excited about what Scotland would have in store for them.

Chapter 7

The castle was far bigger now that they were on the ground than it seemed when they were flying above it in the airship. The walls around the castle were thirty to forty feet tall and, from where they stood, hid the keep that towered several stories behind them.

A tall, dark-haired man in a button-down suit coat and a red and black plaid kilt appeared from around the corner of the castle wall. A woman with long brown hair wearing a white blouse and a matching red and black plaid skirt accompanied him.

With them were a girl and a boy, dressed similarly to the adults, and a gray-haired man in a traditional button-down suit.

Walter MacGregor walked ahead of the group to greet the newcomers.

"Alastair," Walter called, holding his hand out to the man in the kilt.

"Walter," Alastair said, "welcome to Castle MacGregor."

Walter turned to the rest of the party. "This is Lord Alastair MacGregor, the 30th Laird of Castle MacGregor, and his wife, Maeve."

After Walter introduced all the Americans, Alastair said, "These are our children, Mollie and Keir. And this is the Steward of Castle MacGregor, Quinn Montague." The man bowed to them all.

"Please," Maeve said, "welcome to Castle MacGregor. Let us take you inside and you can make yourself at home."

Everyone followed them around the corner of the wall and to the gate of the castle.

"There was a red-haired girl fishing from the drawbridge out here. Is she related to you?" C.J. asked Keir.

"No," the boy said, "she's just a girl from the village." He lowered his voice a bit and added, "She's a bit wild."

"How old are you?" Laura asked Mollie, "I'm twelve."

"I'm sixteen," she responded, but said nothing more.

As they passed under the gateway arch, Scotty pointed out the iron grate with spikes at the bottom, which was suspended over the entrance just outside the wooden gates.

"That's a portcullis," Scotty told them. "They can drop it to help protect the gates against enemies."

"You are correct," Alastair agreed. "luckily, we haven't needed them in many years."

There was another set of gates on the inside of the wall. In the ceiling between the gates, there were several large holes.

"I wonder what those are?" C.J. asked.

"They're murder holes," Scotty replied.

"Correct again," the Lord told them. "They used to shoot arrows down on invading troops. They also dropped rocks or hot sand. Some places even poured boiling oil on some unfortunate armies."

"Ouch," C.J. said.

They crossed through some gardens on the inside of the wall toward the courtyard that led to the keep itself.

"Did castles always have gardens like these?" Sadie asked.

"There were some," Maeve said, "but not as large as these. We don't need so much space for knights anymore, so we expanded our gardens instead."

"Maeve is a horticulturist," Alastair said. "She's in charge of the gardens here."

They crossed the courtyard and entered the castle proper.

The double doors stood open for them as they climbed the few steps and entered the front hall. On one side, a stairway led up to a balcony overlooking the hall.

Several men stood at attention at the side of the hall.

"You are probably tired from your flight," Alastair said. "Quinn will take care of you. Just let him know what you need."

"These men will show you to your rooms," Montague said. "They will bring your luggage up to you from the airship shortly."

C.J. and his Young Explorer friends found that they each got their own room this time. His room was on the third floor of the castle and had a gigantic bed that he could stretch out on in contrast to the compact one he had on the Falcon.

There was also an enormous fireplace in the room, but considering the time of year, they probably wouldn't use it.

He had to share a bathroom, though. It was nestled between his room and Scotty's. It even had a tub with claw feet.

There was a knock on the door and a man appeared carrying C.J.'s suitcase. He laid it on a bench at the foot of the bed and quickly left.

After unpacking, he realized he was a little tired and tried out the bed.

He woke to knocking on his door again. Scotty was outside his door.

"Mom and Dad are going down to look at the excavation," he said. "Do you want to come with us?"

He jumped out of bed and hurried out to the hall. They met Laura and Sadie on the stairs. After asking for directions from one woman dusting the downstairs hallway, they found the door out to a side garden.

The adults were already there surveying the proposed excavation site. They had already set up some equipment in the space, but work had not begun yet. Lord MacGregor was talking to them about his family's plans.

"We're going to create a small patio here," he was saying, "so we are going to clear out a section of the garden."

"What is that?" Angus asked, pointing to a number of large stones stacked up into a pile.

"That's one reason I asked you to come," Alastair said. "We're not sure why anyone would have stacked up stones like that."

"They couldn't have fallen down from a wall that neatly," Walter said.

"Exactly," Alastair said. "Someone placed them there. I'm hoping we'll find out what that reason is."

"When do you start?" Angus asked.

"Now that you are here," Alastair said, "We can get started in the morning."

"Perfect," Edna said. "We'll all be fully rested and ready to start."

"Can we help?" C.J. asked.

"You can watch," Angus told him. "But it will be dangerous moving those stones. You'll have to stay out of the way until that's done."

"It's settled then," Alastair said. "Why don't we go in and have some supper?"

Chapter 8

After breakfast the next morning, everyone gathered in the garden. There were ten laborers that Lord MacGregor had hired to move the stones and the tools necessary to do it lay about the yard.

To move a stone, they laid several round logs out in the direction that they wanted to move the stone. Then several men would use long iron pry bars to lift the stone enough to put the first log under it. Once it was on the log, they would use the pry bars to lift the other end until it rolled along on top of the logs. As logs emerged from the back end of the stone, they moved them in front to continue moving the stone.

They would sometimes have to angle the logs to correct the course of the stone if it drifted away from where they wanted it to end up.

Once it was in position, they would roll it off the logs and use the pry bars to remove the remaining logs, allowing it to settle into its new home.

Sometimes it would take close to an hour to move one stone. Each time they set one stone; they started over with the next one.

Midway through the second stone, the kids lost interest in watching the painstaking work of moving the stones.

"Can we go explore the grounds?" C.J. asked his father.

"If it's ok with Lord MacGregor," Angus said.

"Maybe Keir will show you around the place," Alastair said.

Keir stood and led the way through a set of archways into another garden area. The four kids followed him.

"Have you lived here your entire life?" Scotty asked Keir.

"As long as I remember," Keir told him. "But we didn't live here when my grandfather was Lord MacGregor."

"When did your dad become the Lord of the castle?" Sadie asked.

"About nine years ago when I was three," Keir said.

"What's it like being the son of a Lord?" Laura asked him.

"It's ok. Not much to do," he said.

"What do you do with your friends?" C.J. asked.

"I don't have many friends," Keir told him.

"We're your friends now," C.J. said. "What would you like to do?"

"How about hide and seek?" Laura suggested. "There are lots of places to hide out here."

"That would be fun," Keir said.

"Who's going to be it first?" Sadie asked.

"I will," C.J. volunteered. "Anywhere out here. Not back where they're moving the stones."

The others agreed, and C.J. turned his back on them and started counting. The rest scattered among the tall plants and large stones that littered the ground.

When he reached one hundred, C.J. was off after them.

He checked around the closer boulders, but no one was hiding there. He climbed on one and scanned the area.

He spotted a splash of blue off to one side, but didn't know if that was a flower or the blue of Laura's dress. Running over to it, he found it was indeed just a large blue flower.

He heard someone giggle behind him somewhere and reversed his course toward where he heard the sound. But there was no one there.

He was sneaky and ran behind a column and waited. He counted to ten and then jumped out from behind it again.

He saw some movement by a small boulder in the center of the garden and ran in a straight line to that spot. Jumping over flower bushes and hopping from boulder to boulder, he arrived at the spot just in time to catch Scotty as he tried to flee.

"Caught you," C.J. yelled.

"Aw," Scotty said, laughing. "I almost got away."

"Help me find the others," C.J. told him.

They split up and searched the garden.

C.J. heard a scraping noise from behind a column and leaped around it to catch the person on the other side.

He halted.

The red-haired girl from the drawbridge was sitting with her back to the column, playing with a spinning contraption made of wooden pegs and disks.

"What are you doing here?" he asked her.

"I come here a lot," the girl said. "I like to sit and look at the flowers."

Scotty joined them. "Who's she?" he asked C.J.

"I don't know," C.J. said.

"I'm Greer," the girl told them.

"We're playing hide and seek," Scotty told her. "Do you want to play?"

"Who's we?" she asked.

"C.J. here," he said, "and me. I'm Scotty, by the way."

"Hello," she said.

"Hello," he said. He continued to list off the players. "My sister, Sadie, Laura and Keir, the Lord's son."

"I know Keir," she said.

"What's that?" Scotty asked, pointing at the toy she was holding.

"They're tinker toys," she said. "You can build stuff with them."

"I've heard of those," Scotty said. "Maybe I should get some. I enjoy building things."

Greer laughed. "Sure, I'll play hide and seek. Are the others already hiding?"

"Yes," C.J. said. "I was it. I found Scotty already."

"Ok, give me a minute and then try to find me," she said and darted off around the column.

C.J. and Scotty counted to only thirty this time and ran after her.

They split up again, but Scotty almost immediately said, "I think I see Laura," and ran off to catch her.

C.J. rushed to catch Greer in case she hadn't had time to hide. But there was no sign of her. He ran along the columns of the archway surrounding the garden.

He caught a flash of red hair between two of the columns and darted in that direction. He looked in both directions when he got there, but she was not in view.

Then he saw her standing in front of a column off to the side. He ran right at her, but at the last moment, she jumped out of the way.

He tried to change direction, but his foot caught a stone, and he ran shoulder first into the column and fell to the ground.

Looking up, he saw part of the wall above the archway rock and fall forward down onto him.

Chapter 9

C.J. rolled to the side. He didn't think he'd make it. Suddenly, he felt someone grabbing his arm and leg. They yanked him roughly to the side just as the stone slammed into the ground next to him. He felt a whoosh of air on his face and felt the ground shake as the stone sunk into the soil just inches from his head.

Several smaller rocks pelted him as he covered his head with his arms. One particularly heavy one crashed into his leg.

He yowled as he rolled onto his back and grabbed his leg.

Opening his eyes, he looked up into the wide-eyed faces of Keir and his friends.

"Are you alright?" Sadie asked.

"It could have been worse," he said, glancing at the stone slab next to him. "But my leg aches."

"Let's get you inside," Keir said, offering his hand to the boy. C.J. grabbed it, and they all pulled him to his feet.

"Thanks," C.J. coughed as he brushed the dust off his face. He took a careful step on his injured leg and winced.

"Yikes," he said. "I don't think I can walk on it."

Sadie and Keir helped him through the garden and back toward the castle.

The excavation site erupted into a cacophony of voices when their parents saw them. Everyone wanted to know what happened.

"Are you hurt?" Angus demanded.

"Just my leg," C.J. said.

"A column almost crushed him," Scotty said. "It fell over on top of him."

"What?" Lord MacGregor said.

"It didn't actually fall on top of him," Keir said. "But almost."

"Let's get him up to his room," Maeve said, "I'll call for the doctor."

Alastair called for some men to help take C.J. inside.

When he reached his room, Maeve brought him some water and some pillows to raise his leg.

"The doctor will be here soon," she told him. "For now, just lay back and rest a little." She went downstairs to wait for the doctor.

Angus and the others gathered around the bed.

"Now, what happened?" he asked his son.

C.J. told them the story of playing hide and seek, finding Greer in the garden, and running into the column when he was trying to catch her.

"You do have to watch your step when you are in a seven-hundred-year-old castle," Alastair told him.

"I will next time," C.J. agreed.

Maeve returned with a bearded man carrying a doctor's bag.

"This is Dr. Malcolm," she said.

The doctor placed his bag on a side table.

"What seems to be the trouble?" He asked C.J.

"A rock fell on my leg," he said, pointing to the injury.

The doctor pulled the trouser leg up to expose the bruise on C.J.'s shin. "Hmm, yes, I see," he mumbled. He checked the leg from the boy's knee to his foot.

"Well, it doesn't seem broken," He told them, "But it's swollen. Do you have ice?"

Maeve nodded.

"Wrap some ice in a towel and lay it on the bruise," he told her. Then to C.J. he said, "Keep your leg elevated on these pillows until the swelling goes down. You should be fine in a couple of days."

"Thank you, doctor," Angus said.

"Yes, thank you," Maeve said. She showed the man back downstairs.

Satisfied that C.J. was safe and sound in bed, the other adults went back to the excavation.

"From now on, young man," Angus said, "you watch what you're doing. Be a little more careful around these ruins."

"I will," C.J. told him.

"Now, why don't the rest of us leave him to rest a little?"

Everyone filed out, leaving C.J. alone. He lay back in bed and closed his eyes. In no time, he was asleep.

When he woke a few hours later, he found he was not alone. The red-haired girl was sitting on a chair by the fireplace. Seeing that he was awake, she came over to his bedside.

"Hello, sleepyhead," Greer said.

"What are you doing here?"

"I heard you hurt your leg. I just wanted to see if you were ok."

"Where did you go?"

"I wasn't supposed to be on the grounds," she said, "so when I saw you were safe, I took off."

"Are you supposed to be up here?"

"Not particularly," she said. "So how are you?"

"It's just my leg. A rock fell on it."

"Is it broken?"

"No, just bruised. The doctor said I should be fine in a few days."

"That's good," she said.

They heard footsteps approaching in the hall outside the room. Greer rushed to hide behind the door just as it swung open.

"Just wanted to check on you," Maeve said as she came in. The door swung wide, hiding Greer.

"I'm fine," C.J. said. "I rested for a while."

"Would you like a bite to eat?"

C.J. suddenly felt hungry. "Yes, I would."

"I'll get you a little porridge, and maybe I can put together some cranachan for you."

"Cranachan," C.J. said, "What's that?"

"It's a sweet," she said. "You'll like it."

He hoped so. The porridge didn't sound too promising.

When the door shut, Greer wandered back through the room. "Not too bad a room," she said, "for a castle."

"You'd better go before she gets back."

"Yes, I should. I just wanted to tell you I'm sorry you got hurt." She picked up a bulbous knick-knack from a shelf and looked closely at it. "I didn't want you to get hurt."

C.J. looked at her curiously. "But you want someone to get hurt?"

Greer set the knick-knack back on the shelf. "Oh, no. Why would I want anyone to get hurt?"

"I don't know."

"Well, I better be going," she said. "Maybe I'll stop by again in a day or two."

Without another word, she opened the door and peeked out into the hallway. She slipped out of the room, leaving C.J. staring at the door as it closed.

Chapter 10

In the morning, C.J.'s leg was better, but he still couldn't put his weight on it.

The porridge the night before was better than he feared. It was basically oatmeal with fruit. But the cranachan was fantastic. It was a dessert of raspberries, oats, and cream.

But the breakfast Maeve and Mollie brought up to him out did both. There was a lot of food he didn't recognize, but it included eggs, two types of sausage, bacon, baked beans, mushrooms, and some triangles which the women called tattie scones.

After breakfast, Keir came for a visit. He carried something behind his back.

"I broke my leg when I was ten," he told C.J. "I needed this to walk around for a couple of months."

He produced a well-used pair of crutches.

"They're not in the best shape," he said. "But they should help you get around for the next couple of days."

"Great." C.J. took them and stood up. It took a few tries, but in a few minutes, he could get around the room with little pain.

"Thank you, Keir. This will really help."

"You're welcome," he said with a smile.

C.J. thought it was the first time he had seen him smile. It was probably one of the few times he'd seen anyone in the castle smile. Everyone seemed so serious.

"Do you want to try going downstairs?" Keir asked.

"Sure," C.J. said, "We can see what's going on in the garden."

When the boys arrived in the garden, they found the men were just finishing up moving the second to the last stone. They were about to take a break before attempting the last one.

"Up and about?" Angus asked.

"They're almost done?" C.J. asked.

"They just have that last one," Walter said. "They'll remove it within the hour."

"Then we dig," Jackson said.

"Where's Laura, Sadie and Scotty?" C.J. asked.

"They went into the village to check out what a Scottish village is like," Edna told him.

"Can I go too?"

"If you feel up to it," Angus said, "Come back when you feel tired."

"I will," C.J. said. "Do you want to go?" he asked Keir.

"I'm not supposed to go without my mom or dad," he said, frowning. "One drawback of being a Lord's son."

"Sorry," C.J. told him.

C.J. headed out of the castle and into the streets of Oorlich.

He soon found that the primary mode of transportation in the town was still a horse-drawn cart. There were some back in Minnesota too, but the number of cars out-numbered them.

The people of Oorlich seemed mostly friendly with many answering his "Hello" with an enthusiastic "Hallo". Still, there were a few that scowled at him and ignored his greeting.

When he paused near a gate to a small cottage, an old woman came flying out at him.

"Hey, what are you doing there?" she demanded.

"Just resting a minute," he told her.

"That's my gate," she said. "Go rest somewhere else."

"Sorry."

"Are you one of them that came in that balloon contraption?" she asked.

"Yes."

"And you're visiting the castle?"

"Yes."

"That's a dangerous place to be," she warned him.

"I know." He stuck his injured leg out toward her. "Some ruins fell on my leg."

"No, boy, not the castle itself. The people there."

"The MacGregors?"

"Yes, them," she said. "They're not fit to be friendly with."

"Why not?"

"They're related to Lord Gavin MacGregor himself, aren't they?"

"I don't know who Lord Gavin MacGregor is."

"Was, boy, was. He was a tyrant," she told him, "and a most evil man."

"Was he Alastair MacGregor's father?"

"No. He lived hundreds of years ago."

"But Alastair MacGregor doesn't seem bad to me."

"They all are. Evil runs in the MacGregor veins," she said.

"Well," C.J. said and backed away from the gate on his crutches. "I should be on my way."

"Don't you say that old Morag didn't warn you," the old woman called as C.J. tried to get as far away from her cottage as fast as he could.

He thought she was a strange woman and wondered what she had against the MacGregors.

He ran into his fellow Young Explorers at a small shop with a wooden sign above the door that read Tor's Toys. As they looked through the toys inside, he soon forgot the old woman.

Scotty was looking at some castle building blocks.

"I didn't bring any money," he said.

"Even if you did," Sadie said, "You probably would have dollars, not Scottish pounds or British pounds."

"Pounds?" Scotty asked.

"That's their money," Laura told him. "We have Dollars. They have Pounds."

"You'd have to go to a bank and exchange our money for theirs," Sadie said. "Then you'd be able to buy those."

"Either way," he said, "I can't get them."

They wandered out of the shop and back onto the street.

"Did you see this, C.J.?" Sadie called, pointing to a poster nailed to a wooden post in the middle of the square outside the shop.

"What is it?"

"It says that Lord MacGregor is hosting a celebration at the castle tomorrow night," she said, reading the poster, "to honor the Scottish war veterans."

"Are we invited?" C.J. asked.

"This is the first we've heard about it," Laura said. "Nobody has invited us yet."

A young man appeared in the square and glanced around until he saw them. He rushed up to them.

"Are you the relatives of Lord MacGregor?" he asked.

"We are," Sadie said, pointing at her brother and herself.

"Your father sent me. He has asked that you return to the castle."

"Why?" Scotty said.

"They've discovered something in the garden," he told them.

They rushed back toward the castle, following the man. C.J. on his crutches, tried to keep up with them as best as he could.

Chapter 11

When C.J. arrived in the garden, everyone stood around a pit dug under where the stones had been.

Under several feet of soil was another stone, about seven feet long and four feet wide. It had two words carved into it and the date, 1537. The MacGregors looked concerned.

"What does that say?" C.J. asked them.

Everyone looked at Lord MacGregor.

"It says, Rabhadh Bàs," he said. "I think it might be the name of the person buried under this stone. He probably died in 1537."

There was whispering among the men who helped move the stones from the top of the tomb.

Scotty and Sadie talked excitedly with their mom while Angus conferred with the rest of the adults.

Laura sat on a bench nearby, paging through a book.

"Excuse me. Let me talk to the men privately," Alastair said and joined the other men where they spoke in low tones.

He tried to interrupt his father. "Why are they upset about the tomb?" But his father didn't answer him.

Laura called him over to her.

"Lord MacGregor lied," she told him. "That isn't somebody's name."

"What is it?"

"I thought it sounded familiar. It was a word I read in a Scottish folk tale that I was studying. I had to look it up again, but I found it here." She told him, pointing to a word in her Gaelic dictionary.

"Rabhadh means warning," she said and then flipped the pages to a different word. "Bàs is the Gaelic word for death."

"Warning death," C.J. said. "What does that mean?"

"I don't know," Laura said, "But the others are wondering the same thing."

They couldn't hear what the Lord and workmen were saying, but they were scowling and pointing emphatically at the tomb.

It was over ten minutes later that the discussion broke up. Two men left, but the rest returned to the edge of the tomb with Lord MacGregor.

"Connor and the others have agreed to help lift the stone so that we can see what is under it," Alastair told them. "But they will leave after that."

"Thank you," Angus told them. "We appreciate your help."

The frowning workmen nodded and set to work, preparing to move the stone.

Angus, Jackson, and Walter pitched in to help them.

"What do you think is under there?" Sadie asked her mother.

"I don't know," she said. "It might be a body, as Alastair said."

"He knows that isn't the name of the person," C.J. said.

"What do you mean?"

"Laura translated it. It means 'warning: death'"

"Is that right?" she asked Laura.

"Yes. It was here in this dictionary," Laura said, showing her one entry.

"That's why everyone was upset," Edna said.

"I think they're afraid of whatever is under that stone," C.J. said.

"I wonder why he would lie to us?" She asked.

"Maybe he knows what's down there," Sadie said.

"Alastair," Edna called.

Lord MacGregor looked up from the efforts to get the ropes around the stone. "Yes, Edna?"

"Can I talk to you for a moment?"

He looked down at the men in the pit, hooking up the ropes, and then back at Edna.

"It's important," Edna added.

"Very well," Lord MacGregor said. He had Walter take over his position and came over to where Edna and the kids were standing.

"What do you need?" he asked.

"Do you know what's under that stone?" she asked.

"Why do you ask that?"

"Laura has been studying Gaelic ever since she found out about our trip here," she said, "and she told me that the inscription wasn't the name of someone. It was a warning. And with the way the workmen reacted, I believe her."

Alastair looked at the girl and thought for a moment. Then he sighed. "You're right. It is a warning."

"About what?" Edna asked.

"It's all just superstition, but we Scots are a superstitious lot."

"What's down there?"

"There's a story concerning one of the early MacGregor Lords."

"What kind of story?" C.J. asked excitedly.

"It's said that he condemned a witch to death and beheaded her with his own sword. But before her death, she cursed him and all the MacGregor Lords. She said that they would die by that very sword."

"And did he?" Sadie asked.

"According to the story, that very night they found a knight standing over his body. But it wasn't a human knight. It was his empty armor wielding his sword."

"Oh, my," Edna said.

"His son was so afraid of the knight coming for him he had it entombed somewhere on the grounds of the castle."

"Did you know it was down there?" C.J. asked.

"No, I had forgotten the story completely until I saw the stone," he said.

"Do you believe the story?" Sadie asked.

"No. It was just a legend, like a million other legends of old Scotland. Something used to frighten young children. But now..."

"But now you think it's true?" C.J. asked.

"I don't know. We'll have to see what exactly is under that stone."

They moved closer to the pit and looked down at the men wrestling with the stone covering the tomb.

The ropes were in place and laced through the pulleys attached to a wooden frame erected above the pit.

The men then paused and glanced up at the Lord, waiting for his signal. After a moment, he nodded once, and they all pulled at the ropes.

The stone slowly rose out of the pit. The wooden structure creaked ominously under the weight of the stone, but it held.

Once the stone was above ground level, the men could pivot it slowly until it was no longer over the pit but over solid ground instead.

They let the ropes out and lowered the stone onto the pile of other stones.

They had uncovered the tomb. Everyone looked down at the pit with astonishment.

Chapter 12

A rotten, soiled cloth covered whatever was in the pit. The shape under the cloth was indistinct but roughly the shape of a body. Even if it were the knight, there was more under that cloth than a suit of armor.

"We are done," one worker said. "We opened the tomb, but we are not touching the thing inside it."

"I understand," Lord MacGregor said. "You are free to go."

The man nodded, and the four workers departed.

Jackson looked down into the pit at the covered figure. "Well, I suppose we should get it out of there."

He climbed down in the pit, and soon Angus, Walter, and Alastair joined him. They each grabbed part of the figure and began lifting it out of the pit.

As it moved, there were sounds of metal shifting and clanking. They hefted it until it was almost out when the cloth ripped on the bottom and a sword fell and clattered back down into the tomb.

Walter almost lost his footing in surprise and the body almost slipped out of his grasp.

At the last minute, he regained his balance and readjusted his grip to avoid dropping the figure.

In a matter of minutes, they had it laid out on the ground. Jackson retrieved the sword and placed it on a nearby table.

"There's an insignia on the hilt," he said. "What do you make of it, Alastair?"

Lord MacGregor studied the design imprinted on the sword. "It is an early crest of Clan MacGregor. It has changed over the years, but it certainly belonged to a MacGregor."

"Why was it buried under it?" Angus asked.

Lord MacGregor didn't answer him. He went to the body. "Let's uncover him."

They unwrapped the cloth from the figure. When they were done, they found an unusual sight. It was a full suit of armor, tarnished with age, shackled hand and foot. In addition, there was a chain wrapped around the torso and legs secured with ancient padlocks. They made it so that the arms and legs could not move. However, the padlocks had since rusted and deteriorated until they barely held the chains.

"They didn't want him to go anywhere, did they?" C.J. said.

Lord MacGregor didn't say a word. He kneeled beside the body and examined it intently. He reached out and touched the chains.

His attention shifted to the helmet. He tentatively reached out and put his hand on the visor. He didn't move for a couple of minutes.

"Alastair, are you alright?" Walter asked him.

He said nothing for a moment. "Yes," he said. "I'm not sure what I'm expecting."

"What you're expecting?" Angus asked.

He seemed to take a deep breath and tried to slide the visor up so he could see the face of the man buried in the armor.

It didn't move at first, but he pulled harder, trying to pry it up. With a screech, the rusted hinges gave way, allowing the visor to slide up and reveal the inside of the helmet.

It was empty.

He pulled back his hand from the helmet and clumsily tried to stand up and back away from the armor.

He looked at Edna. "Could it really be true?" he asked.

Edna gaped at the bound armor. "I don't know."

"Is what true?" Angus asked.

Edna recounted the legend of the witch and the death of the Lord by his own armor.

"Do you believe that?" Angus asked Alastair.

"I'm not sure anymore," he said.

"I think we should inspect it," Angus said.

He waved Walter and Jackson over to the armor, and together they removed the chains from it. They placed the chains and the locks to the side for further examination later.

Jackson and Walter examined the plate armor thoroughly.

"This is odd," Jackson said, examining one arm. "There are indentations in the arm's metal where the chains held it."

"There are indentations on the legs too," Walter said.

"Why would the chains dent the armor?" Lord MacGregor asked.

"It's almost like," Angus said. He looked up at the man. "The armor was struggling against the chains."

"Was it trying to get loose?" C.J. asked.

There was a cry, and they all turned to find Maeve had fainted.

They all gathered in a parlor as Edna and Teresa administered smelling salts to Maeve, who was lying on a couch.

"Maeve, are you alright?" Alastair asked.

She was a bit confused at first, but slowly regained composure.

"I'm sorry, Alastair," she said.

"No need to be sorry," he told her.

"Is it true?" she asked, "Is that the armor in the stories?"

"That's just a story. I'm sure it's nothing."

Maeve sat up and drank some tea that Teresa got from the kitchen. She looked at all the faces, looking back at her with concern.

"I'm fine now," she said. "Thank you for the tea."

"Are you sure that you have recovered from your shock?" Alastair asked.

"Yes, dear. No need to fuss over me. I'll just rest here for a bit. You go on with what you need to do."

Alastair nodded to her. "We should probably move the artifacts to a more contained location."

Angus agreed. "Where should we take it?" he asked as the four men headed back to the garden.

"This is a castle," he told them. "There is a dungeon below it. We can lock it up in a room down there."

"Sounds like a good idea," Walter said. "Until we can assess if there is anything to worry about."

When they reached the garden, they all stopped in their tracks. The cloth and the chains lay exactly where they had left them.

But the suit of armor and the sword had vanished.

Chapter 13

"Where could it have gone?" Angus asked.

"Somebody must have taken it," Walter suggested. "Did one man come back after we went inside?"

"They were scared," Alastair told them. "They wouldn't have returned."

"How about your staff?" Angus asked. "Would any of them do something like this?"

"No, I trust them all implicitly."

"Somebody must have taken it," Jackson said. "It wouldn't have walked off on its own."

Everyone fell silent.

"We need to search for it," Angus said. "Jackson, you and Walter search the grounds. Alastair and I will search inside."

They all agreed with his plan and split up to start their search. In a moment, they left the Young Explorers alone in the garden.

"Do you think it just walked off?" Scotty asked.

"No," Sadie said. "That's just a story. Someone is trying to make us believe the curse is real."

"The words on that stone were real," Laura said. "I think there might be something to it."

"What about you, C.J.?" Sadie asked. "Do you think it's real?"

C.J. was on his hands and knees, studying the ground around where the armor had been.

"C.J.?"

"I don't think this knight walked away on its own." he said and pointed to some scratches on the stones leading to the keep. "Someone dragged it inside."

"Let's follow the tracks. We need to find who moved it."

They followed the scratches up to the door. Inside, they could hear Angus and Alastair moving around the main floor, calling out to each other when they had finished searching each room.

C.J. peered at the floor inside the door. There were no scratches.

"They must have come in here," he said. "Fan out and look for some more marks."

The four kids searched the area. It wasn't long before Scotty called from a side hallway.

"I found something," he said.

The four gathered in front of an old door. On the floor were the telltale scratches.

C.J. tried the door. It creaked open, and they found a stairway leading down into the darkness.

"Is that the dungeon?" Scotty asked.

"Could be," C.J. said. He felt around the walls at the top of the steps. "It doesn't look like they had any electric lights installed."

"I've got a flashlight upstairs," Scotty said and ran off to get it.

"Do you think they are still down there?" Laura asked.

"I think we'd see their flashlight," C.J. said, "unless they can see in the dark."

They peered down into the darkness, but they could not make out anything below them.

Scotty returned breathless. "I... got... the... flashlight," he said and handed it to C.J. He stood panting for a moment.

"Go tell Dad we think it's in the dungeon," Sadie told her brother. "And we might need his help."

Scotty nodded and hurried off again.

C.J. shined the flashlight down the steps. Even that light did nothing more than illuminate the steps themselves.

"Well, let's go on down," C.J. carefully started down the stairs.

At the bottom, the stairs opened up into a room with some tables and chairs, as well as several doors. By each door was a large key ring with several keys on each one.

"Three doors," C.J. said, "and three of us."

"I'm not going anywhere by myself," Laura protested.

"We should stay together," Sadie agreed.

They moved to the door directly across from the stairway. C.J. pulled on it and it slowly opened with a low groan from the hinges.

They were about to go through when they heard a thump from somewhere behind the door to the left in the room.

"I guess we're going that way," C.J. said. They moved to that door and listened intently, but there were no additional noises.

C.J. tried the door. Those hinges groaned as well. He shined the light into the hallway beyond the door.

As far as they could see, it was empty. But the light didn't reach very far. The rest of the hallway was in darkness. They took a breath and then stepped into the hallway.

Cell doors lined the hallway, some of them closed and some of them ajar.

Sadie grabbed C.J.'s arm and pointed down the hall. "What's that?" she whispered.

There was light in the distance coming out of one door.

"Turn off the light," she hissed, and pulled C.J. and Laura through a nearby open cell door.

They all held their breath as the light came closer. As the person passed the open door, C.J. almost cried out.

It was Greer.

After she passed, they looked out into the hallway and waited for her light to disappear into the room at the end.

"Quick, let's check out the cell she was in," Sadie said.

C.J. clicked the flashlight back on and they hurried down the hall.

"Here it is," Sadie said, pushing the door open.

C.J. shined the light around the cell, ready for an attack from the knight.

But the room was empty.

"Are you sure this was the one?" Laura asked.

Making their way down the hall first in one direction and then the other, they checked out the cells on either side. They were also empty.

They heard people approaching and saw a light from flashlights bouncing around the hallway. After they hid behind the cell door, they heard a familiar voice.

"C.J.," Angus called. "Sadie. Laura. Are you down here?"

Relieved, they came out of hiding and met their parents and Scotty in the hallway.

They quickly filled them in on how they tracked the armor into the dungeon and saw Greer.

"Which cell did she come out of?" Angus asked them.

When they entered the cell, Angus saw it was empty.

Chapter 14

The next morning, when they gathered for breakfast in the family dining room, they were still talking about the excitement of the night before.

"Why did Greer take the armor?" C.J. asked.

"Did you see her with it?" Alastair asked.

"No, but why else would she be down there?"

"I don't know. She is a little scoundrel. We're always finding her somewhere on the grounds. This is the first time I've heard of her being in the castle, though."

"Uh," C.J. started.

"What?" Angus prompted him.

"She visited me in my room after I hurt my leg," C.J. told him. "She just wanted to tell me she was sorry I got hurt."

"Why didn't you tell us?" Angus asked.

"I didn't think it was important. Sorry."

"Next time," Alastair said. "Please tell us."

"I will."

"We will do a thorough search of the dungeons, but that will have to wait until after the celebration tonight."

"Are we invited to the party?" Sadie asked.

"Well, it's not really a party," Maeve said. "It is more of a ceremony. You are welcome to attend, but you'll need to make sure you stay off to the side and not interrupt it."

"We will," Scotty said.

"You will?" Walter asked. "Stay off to the side or interrupt the ceremony?"

"Stay off to the side," Scotty clarified.

"Good," Walter said.

"People will arrive for the ceremony at around six o'clock this evening," Maeve said. "You'll need more formal attire, but I think we can help you out with that."

Later that day, when C.J. was cleaning up for the ceremony, one of the Lord's men knocked on his door with some clothes for him to wear. It was a shirt, jacket, and kilt similar to what the Lord and Keir were wearing the day they arrived.

He didn't have a problem with the shirt and jacket. Even the bow tie was easy, as he didn't have to tie it.

But he'd never worn a kilt before.

He knocked on Scotty's door.

"Do you know how to wear one of these?" he asked.

"I wore one once," he admitted. "It's not like pants. See these two belts?" He pointed out a belt on either side of the top.

"Yes."

"They tighten it around your belly, not your waist." He lifted his jacket to show how he'd put on his kilt.

"Oh, I see," C.J. said.

He went back to his room and completed dressing for the ceremony.

About a half-hour before six, the four of them gathered on the balcony overlooking the front hall. They felt that would give them a good view of everyone arriving.

While they waited, Laura gave them a lesson in the Gaelic language.

"If you want to greet someone," she told them, "You can say guid eenin. It means good evening."

They each tried to pronounce it with varying degrees of success. Before long, they all could say it decently.

"Look who's here," C.J. said, pointing to the front doors.

A familiar red-haired girl slipped into the hall, shielded from view by a large family who filled the entryway. But from the balcony above, C.J. and his friends could easily track her movements.

She slowly made her way around the room toward the back of the house.

"Do you think she's going to the dungeon?" Scotty asked.

"Maybe," C.J. said. "We need to head her off."

The four of them headed down the stairs and into the crowd. Splitting up, they each made for positions to block her from entering hallways or rooms that were off limits to the ceremony guests.

She hadn't noticed their movements until C.J. stepped in front of her just as she reached the door to the dining hall.

"Hey, Greer," he said cheerfully. "I didn't know they invited you to the party."

"Oh. Hi C.J.," she said, taking a step back. "Yes, I'm here with my family. My father is a veteran of the war."

"Really? Where are they?" he asked, looking over her shoulder at the crowd. "I'd love to meet your parents."

"Oh, I'm sure they're busy talking to their friends somewhere. You'll probably meet them later." She quickly glanced around. "I should probably go find them."

She took off toward another hallway, but they intercepted her again.

"You must be Greer," Sadie said, cutting her off again.

"Who are you?" she said, a little too curtly.

"I'm Sadie MacGregor," she introduced herself. "I'm C.J.'s friend and a relative of the Lord of this castle."

"Oh, hello," she said, glancing around again.

"And that's my brother, Scotty, and our friend, Laura," Sadie said, pointing out the strategically positioned kids.

"I see," Greer said, "and you are what? Watchmen?"

"Of a kind."

"And what are you trying to tell me?"

"You are welcome to come visit us at the castle," Sadie told her. "But come as an official guest and stop sneaking into the castle. It is not your home."

Greer glared at Sadie, who, rather than wilting under her gaze, stood up straighter and leaned closer to Greer.

"We know what you're doing," Sadie whispered.

"Do you?" Greer said and twisted away. She stomped back toward the front gates and disappeared into the crowd.

The other three Young Explorers gathered around Sadie but watched to see if Greer would return.

"She'll be back," Sadie said.

"I'm not sure how we'll keep her out," C.J. told them. "If only..."

A familiar, angry voice rose above the din of the crowd, interrupting C.J. Everyone cut their conversations short and turned to the source of the anger. It was Morag, the old woman who accosted C.J. outside her cottage in the village.

She was standing on a low wall around an indoor planter, lifting her compact frame a little higher above the crowd.

"Lord MacGregor," she repeated. "Where is ye?"

"I'm here, Morag," Alastair said, stepping into the middle of the room in front of her.

The old woman wagged a finger at the Lord and told him. "Be prepared, you villain. You will die this very night!"

Chapter 15

"What are you talking about, Morag?" Lord MacGregor asked her.

"You know very well what's coming for you," the old woman said, glaring down at the man.

"Gavin MacGregor brought this down upon your house," she said, "An evil man he was, but he made the mistake of persecuting a saintly healing woman."

A murmuring started up in the room.

"He struck her down, but not before she cursed him and all the Lords of Castle MacGregor."

"Come now, Morag. Why come here tonight and bother us with this tale of nonsense?"

"It is not nonsense," she growled at him. "It's as true as steel; the steel of the sword."

"What does it have to do with you?"

"That woman was kin o' mine. Your kin killed my kin."

"You said that your kin brought some kind of curse down on the Lords of Castle MacGregor," Alastair told her. "But according to the legend, Gavin was the only one struck down by the curse. That doesn't seem much of a curse."

"It's just been lying dormant for centuries, patiently waiting for the opportunity to rise again."

"Come now, Morag," he said, "get down from there. Let's not interrupt this ceremony any longer. Let's go talk together in private."

"I'd go nowhere private with you," Morag stated, crossing her arms. "You might try to kill me as a witch."

"I agree with you, Morag. By all the stories I've heard and read, Gavin was a tyrant and a loathsome man. But I'm not anything like him."

There were a few shouts of "Here, here" from the crowd listening to the exchange.

"Kin is kin," Morag said.

"Yes, it is," Alastair agreed. "But you say the curse is on all the MacGregor Lords. Not all of us are evil like Gavin was. By calling down the curse on the innocent lords as well as the guilty ones, your kin committed the same sin as Gavin."

"Don't you talk about her like that," Morag screamed.

"Come, Morag. Let go of this ancient hatred. I have no ill will toward you or any of your kin. Hate Gavin all you want, but all I ask is that you let go of this unhealthy malice toward my family. We have done you no wrong."

"Guilt by association," the old woman spat.

"Why, after living peacefully in the village all these years, did you decide to interrupt this celebration tonight with your accusations and indictments?"

"You know why," she said.

"I am at a loss. Has something changed us in your view?"

Quinn Montague stepped up beside the Lord, "Please, Sir. Step away from this. You cannot convince her. I will escort her from the grounds."

"No, Quinn," Lord MacGregor said, "Let her alone." Then he turned back to Morag. "One last time, I ask that you let go of your anger and partake of the festivities and let us celebrate these men and women who fought for us in the Great War."

He bowed to her graciously and turned away.

"You found the knight," she said in a low voice.

He paused for a moment, but then continued to walk away.

"It will come for you," she said louder.

He ignored her and went to the doors of the dining hall. There, he turned and called to the crowd, "Let us enter and feast."

The doors opened and the noise of the crowd returned as they filed in and took their seats at the tables.

Lord MacGregor glanced around, but Morag was nowhere to be seen. He sighed and went back to welcoming his guests into the large hall.

C.J. and the rest of the Young Explorers waited by the door with him, keeping an eye out for the old woman and Greer.

"Greer said she was with her family, but I haven't seen her yet and almost everyone is already seated," he told the others. "I think she was gate-crashing as usual."

"Seems like it," Sadie said. "And where did that old woman go to?"

"She probably left," Scotty said.

Keir came to stand with them. "Hey, why aren't you sitting down yet?"

"We're watching for that girl, Greer," C.J. told him.

"Is she here?" Keir asked, glancing around.

"She was earlier," Laura said. "We're not sure if she still is."

"Let's take ours seats now," Angus said as he passed them and entered the dining hall.

C.J. followed his father to a long table where the other adults were already seated. Each of the kids found a spot near their parents.

C.J. leaned over to his father. "Greer was here earlier. I think she was trying to get to the dungeon."

"Alastair knows," his father told him. "Quinn and his men are standing guard throughout the castle. They're keeping an eye out for her and that old woman."

"How did she know we found the knight?"

"I don't know."

A commotion near the table where Lord MacGregor and his family sat disturbed their conversation. C.J. could see two of the Lord's men struggling with Morag.

The Lord stood. "Morag, I've tried to be patient with you, but I cannot allow you to disturb the ceremony anymore."

He turned to his Steward, "Quinn, please have her removed from the castle."

Quinn signaled to the men, and they tried to guide the uncooperative woman toward the door of the dining hall.

They attempted to be gentle with her, but her struggling required the use of some extra force.

When they arrived at the door, the woman spun around, causing the two men grasping her arms to stumble and almost lose their grip on her.

"The Scottish Knight has finally returned," she shouted across the room. "And with him, so has the curse on the Lords of Castle MacGregor."

Chapter 16

After they removed the woman from the castle, an awkward silence fell over the dining hall.

Sensing he was losing control of the evening, Lord MacGregor stood to get the ceremony back on track.

He started the speech that he had prepared to welcome everyone and to thank the veterans there for their service, and the families of the veterans they lost for their sacrifice for their country.

He then introduced the Army General, who was in command of the troops from their part of the country. The General gave his own tribute to those present.

After introducing several more speakers, Alastair soon completed the ceremony.

Lord MacGregor stood once more and thanked everyone for attending and wished them all a good night.

Those who had finished their meals filed out and returned home. Others continued to eat and talk with friends and comrades.

When the last guest had gone, they locked up the castle. Alastair and his family retired to a nearby study with his guests.

"Do you think either of them is still in the castle?" Angus asked him.

"Quinn and the men are searching now," he said, accepting a glass from Maeve. "We should hear their report soon."

"Do you think Greer told Morag about the knight?" C.J. asked.

"I'm sure she did," Alastair said. "Greer is Morag's granddaughter."

"She is?" Sadie said, leaning forward in her chair.

"Yes," Maeve said. "The poor girl lost her parents in the war. Her father was a cavalry officer who died in battle. Her mother was an army nurse. She died when the hospital she was working in was shelled."

"She came to stay with her grandmother during the war and has been here ever since," Alastair said.

"Poor girl," Edna said. "Do you think she believes in this curse?"

"I don't know," Alastair said. "If she took the armor, she might."

"Or she wants us to believe it," Walter said. "Either way, we can't trust her."

There was a knock on the door, and Quinn entered.

"We finished locking up and searching the castle," he reported. "No sign of the woman or the girl."

"Did you look in the dungeon?" C.J. said.

Quinn raised his eyebrow at the question.

Alastair smiled. "Yes, did you look in the dungeon?"

"Indeed," Quinn said. "No sign of anyone in the dungeon, not even a knight."

"Just curious," C.J. said, blushing.

"Thank you, Quinn," Alastair said. "You and the men can retire."

Quinn bowed and left the room.

"We should all retire," he said. "It's been a long day."

"And tomorrow may be a long day too," Angus added, "if we are to find that knight."

"Yes," Alastair agreed, "it will be."

After the excitement of the day, C.J. fell right to sleep as soon as he got into bed. His dreams were full of knights and battles.

He awakened to the sound of a crash, but he wasn't sure if it was part of his dreams.

Sitting up in the bed and listening, he heard some footsteps in the hallway outside. After a moment, there was a tap on his door.

When he opened the door, he found Scotty outside.

"Did you hear that?" Scotty asked.

"A crash?"

"Yes, I think it was downstairs."

There was a shout from several men downstairs. There was another crash somewhere above them, followed by a scream.

C.J. quickly dressed and rejoined Scotty in the hallway. When he stepped into the hall, he saw men running upstairs.

"What's going on?" he asked.

"I don't know," Scotty said. "Did you hear a scream?"

Before C.J. could answer, they heard another scream from the floor above them. They raced for the stairs.

Men were shouting somewhere above them as they climbed the stairs.

When they reached the top, they could see the doors to the Lord's suite had been battered in. Two men lay on the floor on either side of it. C.J. could see that they were bleeding.

When they reached the door, the knight appeared in the doorway, a bloody sword held in his hand.

"Run," C.J. yelled to Scotty.

Scotty ran. C.J. headed for the stairs again. He looked back and found the knight was chasing after him.

When he reached the top of the stairs, he saw several men running from the door after the knight.

He ran down the stairs, but the knight quickly gained on him. Glancing back, he could see the knight raising the sword above him.

Thinking quickly, he stopped abruptly and ducked to the side, hoping the knight's momentum would carry him past.

It almost worked. The swing of the sword missed, but the arm of the knight collided with his shoulder and sent him against the railing. It knocked the wind out of him and he collapsed on the steps.

The knight continued down the stairs with the guards trailing after him. One guard stopped briefly to make sure he wasn't injured too badly before he followed the others.

"C.J.!" Scotty yelled from the top of the stairs.

"I'm ok," C.J. said. He saw that Sadie and Laura were with Scotty.

He heard other voices above him.

"Father," Keir called.

C.J. reached the top of the stairs in time to see Maeve grab the boy and prevent him from entering the suite. He saw she had blood on her nightgown.

Mollie came running from down the hall. Maeve swept her up in an embrace with her and her son.

"Where's father?" she demanded.

"You can't go in there," Maeve told them.

"Where is he?" Keir repeated.

"He's gone," Maeve told them, tears in her eyes.

"Gone?" Mollie said.

"Yes," Maeve said, and they all broke down.

Moments later, the men returned from downstairs.

"Did you find it?" Maeve asked. "No, M'Lady," one said. "It was like it just disappeared."

Chapter 17

C.J. and Sadie helped their parents check on the men who had fallen by the door to the Lord's suite. They were bleeding from several wounds, but they quickly staunched those with the help of bandages Quinn brought. None of their injuries were life-threatening.

"Are you injured?" Quinn asked Maeve.

"No," she said, looking down at the blood on her nightgown. "The blood is not mine."

"I have summoned the police and the doctor," Quinn said.

"Yes. Good." She looked at her children sitting on the floor beside her.

"Can you both go to Mollie's room?" she told them. "I need to change."

They nodded and headed back down the hallway.

"I'll be there in a few minutes," Maeve called after them.

When they were gone, Maeve spoke to Quinn.

"They can't see their father like that. I'll keep them in Mollie's room until the doctor can remove his body."

"Very well," Quinn said. "As soon as the police are done, we will clean up the room as best as possible."

"Thank you," she said.

Quinn returned downstairs to wait for the authorities.

"If there is anything we can do for you and your children," Angus told her, "Just say the word."

"I appreciate your offer," she said. "I just have to be there for Mollie and Keir."

"Of course."

After Maeve entered the bedroom to change, she attempted to close the doors as well as she could. But they hung at odd angles with some hinges broken.

"How is your shoulder?" Scotty asked C.J.

"What's wrong with your shoulder?" Angus asked him.

"The knight whacked him when it chased him down the stairs," Scotty said.

"Let me look at it," Angus said, rolling up C.J.'s sleeve. The boy's upper arm was red, but there was no bruising. "How does it feel?"

"It hurts. But it's not too bad."

Quinn returned with several police officers and Dr. Malcolm, who had treated C.J.'s leg.

"The Lord is in the bedroom here," Quinn told them.

They heard someone pushing on the door, but it wasn't opening. Quinn rushed over and helped Maeve out of the room. She had put on a dark dress.

"M'Lady," one police officer greeted her, "I am Chief Constable Hutton. I'm very sorry about Lord MacGregor."

"Thank you."

"If possible, I would like to speak with you later."

"Yes, of course. I'll be in my daughter's room."

"Very good, Ma'am."

The Chief Constable gave a slight bow to her as she turned and headed down the hall. He then directed his men to enter the bedroom and begin the investigation.

"Come with me, Doctor," he said, escorting the physician through the doors into the bedroom.

Angus drew his son aside. "You saw the knight?"

"Yes. He was right beside me."

"Could you tell if someone was in the armor?"

"You think a person killed him, not the curse?"

"That would be the most likely case."

C.J. stared at the floor in thought for a minute. He rubbed his arm absentmindedly.

"I really couldn't tell," he said, his attention back to his father. "The visor was down so that I couldn't see a face. And the armor covered the rest of him. Sorry."

"No need to be sorry," Angus said. "I doubted you could tell."

He looked around at their little group of parents and kids outside the bedroom. "Why don't we all leave them to their work and go downstairs to the study? I'm sure they will also want to talk to us later."

It was some time before the police officers finished their investigation in the Lord's bedroom. But after they had, two of them appeared at the study's door.

"We would like to take your statements now," one told the group.

One by one, everyone in the room gave their statements to the police officers. While everyone had their own story about where they were and what they saw of the knight, no one mentioned anything about the curse or whether someone was in the suit of armor.

When the questioning was done, they asked one last question to the entire group. "Did anyone see what happened to this knight?"

"It went downstairs," C.J. said. "Some men ran after it, but none of us saw it again."

They closed their notebooks. "Thank you for your cooperation. If we have any more questions, we will contact you."

"Thank you," Angus said.

When they opened the study door to leave, C.J. could see two men carrying a stretcher up the stairs.

"They're going to bring Lord MacGregor's body down," he told the others.

The four kids hurried out into the front hall to watch for him. Their parents soon joined them.

Several other men were setting up a table in the front hall. They placed one long one toward the back with candles on the ends.

It wasn't long before the men with the stretcher were making their way back down the stairs, carrying Lord MacGregor. They had strapped his body to the stretcher, and a sheet covered him. Two of Quinn's men joined in, helping guide it down the steps.

When they reached the bottom of the steps, they took the stretcher to the long table. They unstrapped the body and lifted it onto the table.

When they removed the sheet, it surprised C.J. to see that they dressed the man in his formal attire.

They arranged him on the table with his hands folded on top of him. They placed a pipe in his hands and a tobacco bowl beside his body.

The men stopped and stood by as if guarding him.

Maeve made her way down the steps and over to her husband. She stood and gazed down at his face.

There was no visible injury to the man. He looked as he had the night before. But his eyes were closed, and his face was slack.

She touched his cheek and gazed down at him for several minutes. Tears filled her eyes.

She placed a hand on the top of his head. "Goodbye, my love," she said, barely audible.

Chapter 18

Maeve and her children had breakfast in the front hall in the morning. People from the village filed into the hall quietly throughout the morning. They would stop and pay their respects to Lord MacGregor, stop at his family's table to offer their condolences, and then wander off to get a drink and a bite to eat.

Visitors took turns watching over Lord MacGregor while others used pipes provided by the family and smoked the tobacco left for them by the Lord's body.

Quinn came to Walter and Edna's table.

"I would like to extend M'Lady's apologies for not joining you this morning."

"No need to apologize," Angus told him. "She is busy with guests."

"I agree," Walter said. "Please let her know we will do whatever we can to help her in this dreadful time."

"I will tell her," Quinn said. "I also wanted to let you know we are still searching for the knight."

"Thank you for telling us," Angus said. "Hopefully, they find it soon."

"Yes," Quinn said. "Now I'll leave you to finish your meals."

After Quinn left, silence fell again over the meal.

After a while, Walter broke the silence.

"I'm sorry that we won't be able to get to know Alastair better," he said. "He seemed like a good man."

"He was," a voice said. Everyone turned to find Maeve standing at their table.

Everyone rose.

"Please," Angus said, "would you sit with us?"

"I would like that," Maeve said, "but only for a few moments."

Angus and Walter held her chair for her as she sat down. A young woman appeared out of nowhere with a plate of food and a goblet of water.

"Thank you," Maeve said.

"How are you holding up?" Walter asked.

"As well as anyone can expect," she said. "Only time will tell."

"And your children?" Angus asked.

"They have been quiet," she said. "Their world has just turned upside down."

"Yes, it has," Angus said. He put his arm around C.J. and hugged him. "We lost C.J.'s mother several years ago."

"I'm so sorry," Maeve told them.

"Thank you," Angus said. "It was a tough time for both of us. The sadness never quite disappears, but it will eventually become bearable. You and your children will also have some tough times ahead. But you'll see glimpses of him in something your children say or do and realize that he lives on in them."

She looked from Angus to C.J. and thought for a moment.

"I appreciate the thought," she said. "It feels like a long way off."

"I know," Angus said. "Just know you will make it through this."

"Excuse me," C.J. interrupted. "Would it be all right if Sadie, Scotty, Laura, and I sit with Mollie and Keir?"

"You are welcome to," Maeve said. "They just might like the company."

The four kids excused themselves and headed to Mollie's and Keir's table.

When they got there, they discovered the table had a guard posted. He came to attention as they approached.

"Their mother said we could sit with them if they liked," Sadie told him.

The guard looked at the pair, and Mollie nodded. "You are welcome to sit," he told them, waving to the empty chairs.

Keir had a blanket wrapped around himself while Mollie gazed out toward one of the large windows in the hall.

Sadie immediately went to Mollie and embraced her. Laura went to Keir and sat in the chair next to him. She hugged him as well as she could through the blanket.

C.J. and Scotty took their seats across the table from the others.

"We are so sorry about your dad," Sadie told Mollie. "If there is anything we can do."

"I don't know," Mollie said, hugging her back. "How can we even know what to think right now?"

"Do you just want to talk?"

"I don't know what to say."

"That's how I felt when I lost my mom," C.J. said. "Everyone was nice to me, but I was just sort of...." He thought for a moment. "Lost, I guess."

"That's how I feel," Keir said. "I don't know what to do."

"Right now, you don't have to know," C.J. told him. "When my mom died, my dad just told me where to go and what to do. I didn't have to decide."

"How did your mom die?" Mollie asked.

"She had cancer."

"That's awful. I'm sorry."

"After she died, there were so many relatives and visitors that I didn't have time to let myself feel sad until after the funeral."

"We won't get a chance even then," Mollie said.

"Why?" Sadie asked.

"After the funeral, a ceremony passes the title down to Keir. He will be the new Lord MacGregor," Mollie said.

"I thought you would be next in line," Sadie said, confused. "You're the oldest."

"That's not how it works," Mollie said. "The title goes to the oldest son. It would only go to the oldest daughter if there weren't any sons."

"How do you know what to do as Lord MacGregor?" Scotty asked Keir.

"I don't," Keir said, pulling his blanket tighter around him. "Mother will take care of things until I'm old enough and learn what to do."

"Being a Lord is not as much fun as you'd think," Mollie said. "There's a lot of responsibilities and traditions to uphold. It's a lot of work."

"And what's worse," Keir said, pulling the blanket over his head until just his eyes and nose were peeking out. "If I'm Lord MacGregor, the knight will be after me."

"Oh, no," Sadie said with her hand over her mouth. "I didn't think about that. What are we going to do?"

"There's only one thing we can do," C.J. said. "We have to figure out a way to stop the knight."

"How?" Mollie asked.

"I don't know yet. There must be some way to stop it or remove the curse," C.J. said.

"I hope so," Keir said. "I don't want to die."

Chapter 19

The morning of Lord MacGregor's wake was sunny and warm. A trickle of people stopped by throughout the night to show their respects to the fallen man.

The staff served breakfast as soon as the sun rose.

Quinn stopped by to let Walter, Edna, and the others know the schedule for the day.

"The wake will continue this afternoon," he told them. "Eventually, most everyone in the village will attend."

"What about Morag?" Angus asked.

"We are on the lookout for her," Quinn said. "Hopefully, she will stay away."

"What about the burial?" Walter asked.

"That will be here at the castle. There is a family cemetery on the grounds here. It will be tomorrow after the wake ends."

"Are you expecting a crowd for that as well?" Edna asked.

"No, that will be a private ceremony. Only family, castle staff, and special guests."

"Are we special guests?" C.J. asked.

"Yes, of course," Maeve said, as she and her children passed by, making their way to their table.

She glanced out the window at the few clouds floating by.

"Such a bright and cheery day. I wonder what tomorrow will be like," she said. "It seems ironic to bury Alastair on a beautiful day like this."

"It's trying to lift your spirits," Edna said.

Maeve nodded. "It's not working," she said.

"I understand," Angus said. "You need to feel what you need to feel. Nature can't change that."

Maeve glanced around the table and noticed the children had finished their breakfasts. "You don't need to keep us company if you've finished eating."

C.J. looked at his father for permission to leave the table. His father nodded to him. He and the other Young Explorers rose to leave.

"I'm not hungry," Keir said. "Can I go with them?"

"Of course," Maeve told him.

The five kids went outside the castle.

"What do you want to do?" C.J. asked Keir.

"I don't know," he told them.

"Let's find out where that knight went," Scotty said.

"That's a great idea. I'm in," Sadie added.

"Me too," Laura said.

"We can do that," Keir said.

They spent the next several hours searching the castle. Eventually, they descended the stairs to the dungeon and the room they had seen Greer leave. It was as empty as it was that night.

"This was the room?" Keir asked.

"Yes, I'm sure it was," Sadie told him.

C.J. started checking for marks on the floor that showed the knight had been there, but he and Keir found nothing.

Laura and Sadie systematically moved around the room, stomping on the floor, and knocking on the stone walls, looking for secret doors. Everything sounded solid.

Scotty stood in the center of the room, staring at the walls. He would look at one wall, then another, and then back at the first. "Hmm," he said to himself.

"What is it?" his sister asked him.

"I don't know," he said. "Something seems off, but I can't put my finger on it."

The others looked at the walls with him but noticed nothing unusual.

"Scotty!" someone called from down the hall. "Sadie!"

Sadie went out into the hallway and found her mother looking for them.

"It's time to go back upstairs," she said.

"How did you know we were down here?" Sadie asked.

"I know you," she said. "You will not rest until you find out where that knight went."

"You definitely know us," C.J. said.

"Find anything?" Edna asked.

"Not a thing," Scotty said.

"You can try again later," His mother told him. "But now, we have to get back to the wake."

When they returned to the hall, all the activities amazed them.

In one corner were some bagpipers playing a song with a woman singing in Gaelic. It was a lively tune that seemed incongruous with the fact that they were there mourning a man's death. People around them were clapping in time with the song.

Another group was playing Blind Man's Buff with a blindfolded young man, trying to catch people from a crowd around him.

C.J. suspected the man could see around the edge of the blindfold because he kept trying to catch only the young ladies in the crowd.

Several tables of people were playing various card games. There was even a group playing cards at the table where Lord MacGregor was lying in state. They had dealt a hand to the man himself and took turns playing for him.

Other people were playing more physical games. Some gathered around a table where two burly men were arm wrestling. Others held a stick in front of themselves and tried jumping over it. Another group cheered on a pair of men who were sitting on stools. They were taking turns trying to slap the other off their seat.

The Young Explorers had not been to many funerals, but the carnival atmosphere seemed strange and surreal.

The festivities lasted long into the evening, and as the hours wore on, the games and conversation became quieter, and the crowds diminished.

It was late when their parents sought them out and told them it was time to retire for the night.

"I wanted to stay until it was over," C.J. said.

"It won't be over until tomorrow," Angus told him. "Some people will be here all night."

"Have you ever been to a wake like this before?" Sadie asked her parents.

"No," Edna said. "I've heard about these remembrances in Scotland and Ireland. But we haven't been to one before. Different traditions like this are interesting to experience."

"But it's weird," Scotty said.

"It might be weird to us," Walter said. "They would find our funeral traditions to be weird, too."

"But now, off to bed," Angus said.

The kids slowly ascended the stairs while checking what was happening below them. When they reached the balcony overlooking the hall, C.J. and Scotty stopped at the rail while Sadie and Laura continued up the stairs.

C.J. saw his father wave him on again, so he and Scotty went upstairs to their rooms for the night.

He wondered what strange traditions they would experience at the funeral the next day.

Chapter 20

By the time C.J. and his friends came down the following day, the last villager had been long gone, and the only people left in the front hall were two of the castle staff guarding Lord MacGregor's body.

Staff removed most of the tables and restored the hall to its pre-wake state. The kids cut through the hall and headed to the family's dining room to find breakfast and the rest of their families.

The adults were already there when they arrived, but breakfast had not yet been served. Maeve and her children hadn't come down to breakfast either.

"Is the wake over?" C.J. asked.

"Not officially," Walter told him. "It ends when they take his body out for the funeral."

"When's that?" Sadie asked.

"Early this afternoon," Edna said. "Now, sit down. Breakfast will be in shortly."

"Actually, right now, if I am not very much mistaken," Jackson said as the door to the kitchen opened, and several women swept into the room carrying plates of food.

"What about Mrs. MacGregor?" Laura asked.

"She and the kids were up late," Edna told them. "They won't be up until shortly before the funeral."

"What should we do until then?" C.J. asked.

"I wanted to learn more about Gavin MacGregor," Laura said. "I was going to see if they had anything in their library about him."

"That sounds like a project for you," her mom said. "Maybe all of you can look through the books."

"I wonder if they have any books about this castle," Scotty said.

"Maybe," Edna said. "You can always look."

The four Young Explorers quickly finished breakfast and returned to the front hall.

"I saw the library down this way," Laura said, heading down a side hall.

She stopped in front of a pair of ornate wooden doors. "This is my favorite room of all I've seen in this castle," she said as she pushed the doors open.

The room was two stories tall, with the walls lined with bookshelves. A walkway around the walls gave access to books higher on the shelves. A ladder in two corners led up to the walkway.

The center of the room had several heavy wooden tables and chairs where you could sit and read books. Four windows cut into the bookshelves allowed enough light during the day to read comfortably.

Laura walked around the room, glancing at the books on the shelves. "They must have organized the books somehow," she told them.

The four of them fanned out to examine the books.

"These books look like they are all about gardening," Scotty said, standing before one bookshelf. "But most of them are in some other language."

"I'm sure it's probably Gaelic," Laura said.

As they moved about the room, they discovered books about Scottish history and poetry, novels, and even a whole bookshelf of encyclopedias.

It wasn't long before Scotty found a section about castles and architecture. The four searchers then became three.

They climbed the ladders and investigated the second level.

The books on that level were noticeably older, and their hopes of finding something about the earlier Lord of MacGregor castle rose.

Many older books had faded covers, and they had to pull a few out of each section to determine what they were about. Laura had learned enough Gaelic to get the gist of the subject of many books, but some required her to look up words in her dictionary.

Time was ticking away. They would soon need to go to the funeral, but they hadn't yet discovered anything about the MacGregor family.

"This might be something," Sadie called from a corner bookcase. Stacks of journals lined the shelves. Each handwritten journal had dates marked on each entry.

"See if you can find any dated around the early 1500s," Laura told them. "That is the time of Gavin MacGregor."

They started pulling the journals off the shelves. After quickly paging through a book, they would stack it with the others on the floor.

One pile became another and then another, but none of the journal dates were of that period.

Soon, they had sorted all the journals in the bookcase except for a few on the top shelf. Unfortunately, they needed to be taller to reach those.

C.J. looked around the catwalk but saw no ladders that could reach the top shelves.

"I've got an idea," Sadie said. "It might be sacrilegious to use old books like this, but...." She rearranged the journals and stacked four large, solid books on the floor before the shelves.

"Spot me," she told the others and carefully stepped up on the journals, holding onto a shelf to steady herself. She grabbed one volume at a time and handed it off to C.J. and Laura. When she was done, she jumped down off the stack.

They quickly leafed through the journals until Laura let out a whoop. "Gavin signed these entries."

C.J. and Sadie crowded around Laura as she paged through the book. Soon she came to the last pages, dated the year 1537.

"His last entry says," Laura told them and then read haltingly as she translated, "I finally took revenge on the witch that killed my wife. It is done."

"He wrote no more after that?" C.J. asked.

"No, the next entry is by his son, Euan," she said. "My father is dead. The knight from the witch's curse killed him. We imprisoned the knight in the garden before it could come after me."

"Is that it?" Sadie asked.

"There is one more dated three days later," Laura told her. "I sit in the garden by the stones, and the sound I hear daily in that spot chills my heart. The thumping sound of the knight fighting against its prison. I worry that someday, it might escape."

Chapter 21

"We let it escape," Laura said. "And it killed Lord MacGregor."

"We helped," Sadie said, "But Lord MacGregor brought us here to help excavate that area. None of us knew it was down there."

"We can't do anything about what's happened," C.J. said. "All we can do is try to stop the knight and the curse."

"How do we do that?" Laura asked.

"Sadie!" a voice called from the hallway. "Scotty!"

Scotty went to the hallway door. "We're here, Mom."

Edna MacGregor met Scotty at the entrance to the library and glanced around for the other kids. She saw they were up on the catwalk. "Come on down, you three," she told them. "It's nearly time for the funeral."

"We'll be right down," Sadie called to her. The three quickly replaced the books on the shelves and climbed down the ladder.

"Change back into your formal outfits," she told them as she shooed them out of the room.

It didn't take them long to change, and they were back in the front hall waiting for their parents. Lord MacGregor was no longer lying on the table. In his place was a coffin.

"Is he in there?" Scotty asked in a whisper.

"I would think so," Sadie whispered.

Their parents soon joined them.

"When does the funeral start?" Scotty asked.

"Any time now," Walter told them. "We're just waiting on Lady MacGregor and her children."

Several men and a priest entered the front hall and took their places on both sides of the coffin. They stood waiting.

It wasn't long before Maeve, Mollie, and Keir descended the steps to the hall. Maeve held a small bouquet of purple flowers.

The priest visited with her, and when she indicated they were ready, he moved to the coffin and signaled the men to begin.

They lifted the coffin and followed the priest toward the back of the castle. Maeve and her children followed them.

C.J. and the other kids walked behind their parents in the back of the procession.

When they reached the cemetery behind the castle, the men carrying the coffin had already placed it on wood beams over an open grave.

Maeve and her kids stood beside the coffin while several castle staff gathered around the group. She clutched the bouquet in her gloved hands.

The four kids stood in a group with their parents on the opposite side of the coffin from the MacGregors.

The priest began the service with a prayer and followed it with some words about Lord MacGregor.

C.J. wasn't listening. Scotty, who stared at the beams under the coffin, distracted him.

"Wooden beams," Scotty mumbled. "Wood beams."

Edna shushed him, but he stared off into space, thinking.

The service did not last very long and was soon over. The priest briefly visited with Maeve before he left.

One by one, the staff stopped and gave their condolences to the three MacGregors before returning to work.

The men who carried Lord MacGregor to the cemetery gathered two coils of rope. After consulting with Maeve, they fed the rope under the coffin, and while they held the ropes tight, one man removed the beams from under it.

Slowly, they let the ropes out, and the coffin descended into the open grave. Once it came to rest on the bottom, they pulled the ropes out.

Maeve moved to the edge of the grave and looked down at her husband's last resting place. With a sob, she threw the bouquet down onto his coffin and returned to her kids.

With a nod from Maeve, the men filled the grave.

Angus and the other parents went to Maeve and offered her and her kids a few words of sympathy before she returned to the castle.

The adults followed her into the castle, leaving the four kids in the cemetery, watching the men fill the grave.

"What were you mumbling about?" C.J. asked Scotty.

"Mumbling?" Scotty asked.

"You said something about wood beams," C.J. reminded him.

Scotty thought about that. "Oh yeah," he said, "The wood beams under the coffin reminded me of something, but I couldn't remember what it was."

"Something important?" Sadie asked.

"I think so," Scotty said, "I just couldn't remember where I'd seen them before."

"Those wood beams?" Laura asked.

"Not those exactly," Scotty said, "Some other ones."

"Let's go back to the castle," Sadie said.

They all agreed.

They found their parents seated in the study inside the castle just off the front hall.

"Where's Lady MacGregor?" Sadie asked.

"She and the kids have gone to petition the House of Lords to confer the title on Keir," Edna said. "I wouldn't expect them to return for a few days."

"Mollie said there will be a ceremony to introduce Keir as the new Lord MacGregor," C.J. said. "How soon is that?"

"I don't know," Walter said. "Maybe in a couple of days."

"We need to find that knight before he becomes Lord," Sadie said.

"They have been searching for it," Angus told them. "We don't know where it is hiding."

"Hiding," Scotty said, then repeated, "Hiding."

"You're mumbling again," Edna told him.

"Again?" Scotty asked.

"Yes, you were mumbling to yourself during the funeral."

"About wood beams," C.J. reminded him.

"Wood beams?" Scotty said, "Yes, wood beams." The boy leaned back in his chair and stared at the ceiling.

"He's off again," Sadie said, laughing.

"Scotty does that a lot," Edna said. She smiled at her son.

Suddenly, Scotty jumped up from his chair. "Wood beams!" he shouted. "That's it." He pointed up at the walls of the study. The ends of wood beams poked out of every wall.

"What about them?" C.J. asked.

"They hold up the ceilings," Angus said.

"Normally, they do," he said. "But I wondered what they were doing there." He paced around the room, waving his arms wildly. "They shouldn't have been there."

"They shouldn't have been where?" Walter asked. Scotty stopped pacing. "I think I know where the knight is hiding," he said, running out of the study.

Chapter 22

Everybody sat and looked at each other in confusion, and then they all jumped up to follow the boy.

When they reached the front hall, Scotty was not in sight.

"Scotty," Walter called, "Where are you?"

His voice came from down the hallway toward the back of the castle. "I'm back here."

"Back where?" Walter said as they all set off after him.

"The dungeon," he called.

When they reached the door to the dungeon, it was open, but the steps down were in darkness, and there was no sign of Scotty.

"He must have taken the flashlight down," C.J. said.

"Are there any lights down there?" Angus asked.

"No," Sadie said.

"Is there another flashlight?"

"I'll see if I can get one," Walter said and hurried toward the kitchen, where the staff was busy preparing dinner.

"Do you have any idea what Scotty is up to?" Edna asked Sadie.

"No," she said. "I don't know what those wood beams have to do with anything down there."

"Should we get Mr. Quinn?" Laura asked.

"Let's see what Scotty finds before we bring him into it," Edna said. "He might have something, or he might not."

Walter returned with several flashlights and passed them out to the adults. "Let's go find him," he said.

They descended the steps down to the main room on the lower level.

"Where do you think he went?" Angus asked.

"This way," C.J. said, heading to the door on the left.

Everyone followed him through the door, the flashlight beams bouncing around the hall ahead of them.

They found the boy in the cell they had been in several times before.

"See," Scotty said, pointing at the two wooden beams poking through one wall by about two feet. "Why are they there?"

"To hold up the ceiling like everywhere else," Walter told him.

"Then why only that wall?" Scotty said. "The last time we were down here, I knew there was something different about that wall than the other three. Upstairs, I realized it was the wooden beams."

"Ok," Angus said. "Then why are they there?"

Scotty went out into the hall with C.J. in pursuit. He followed Scotty down the hall to the next cell door. When they entered that cell, the wood beams were sticking out on that side of the wall just as far as in the other cell.

"They're only a few feet long," C.J. observed.

"Wait a minute," Scotty said and returned to the hallway. They met the rest of their group out there.

"Do you notice something?" Scotty asked C.J.

Everyone looked confused.

"Look at the distance between those two cells," Scotty said, pointing at the two doors.

"There's plenty of space for another cell, but there isn't a door," C.J. said.

"There must be a secret door into that room from that first cell," Scotty said.

"We checked all the walls the first time we were there," Sadie said. "They were all solid."

"There must be one," Scotty said, rushing into the cell again.

When the rest of them entered the cell, they found him peering up at the beams. "It must have something to do with them," he said.

C.J. and Sadie rechecked the walls under the beams. They pounded the stones, but they all sounded solid. They tried pushing them, but none of them moved.

Finally, they searched the masonry around the stones for any holes where a latch could hide, but, except for some cracks commonly found in stone walls, they found nothing unusual.

"Are we sure there is a secret door?" Sadie asked.

"There must be," Scotty said. "Why else would Greer pick this cell?"

"And why would there be such a large space between the cells?" Angus agreed.

"Is there a hole above that one?" Edna asked.

When they looked closer, the beam had a slot several inches high above it. The stone above it was not sitting on it at all.

"See if there is a release in the slot," Scotty said.

Although it was high on the wall, Jackson was tall and could reach the hole. He felt around inside but found nothing.

"It's just a hole," he told the others.

"There must be some way...." Scotty said. He stared down at his hands. He moved his fingers as if trying to figure out how the mechanics of the secret door would work.

"Wait a minute," he said, moving his hand like lifting something. "Yes," he said, raising his hand again. "That could work."

He turned to Jackson. "Push up on the beam," he told him.

Jackson looked at the others. Angus shrugged and nodded to him. He stood under the beam and pushed up on it. It rose until it met the stone above it.

"Now push," Scotty told everyone else. C.J. and Sadie pushed on the wall below the beam. The wall pivoted inward with a slight grinding noise, revealing a dark space.

"Step back," Angus told the kids. He and Walter slipped past Jackson as he let the beam drop back into place.

They entered what appeared to be another cell. The beams stretched across the room's ceiling to the opposite wall, and a dark rust color stained the floors.

"Blood?" Walter asked.

"Ancient blood," Angus agreed. "An old torture chamber?"

They shined the flashlights around the room until they glinted on something metal in the corner.

"What did you find?" Edna called.

"Just like Scotty told us," Walter told them.

The kids ran into the hidden room to see what was in it.

The knight stood at attention in the corner, lit by flashlights.

"Scotty found where the Scottish Knight is hiding," his father said.

Chapter 23

"Get out of there," Teresa told them. "It's not safe."

"It's not moving," C.J. said.

"Maybe not right now, but it killed before."

"She's right," Walter said, "All of you out of here."

The kids reluctantly went back into the outer cell.

"Go get Quinn and his men," Angus told Jackson. "Let him know we found the knight."

"Right away," Jackson said as he headed out the door and back up to the main level of the castle.

"Do you think it will try to kill Keir?" C.J. asked his dad.

"We don't know," Angus said. "Keir doesn't technically have the title yet."

"But he will soon."

"And we hope to have the knight secured before that," his dad assured him.

"How?"

"They had it chained before, and that seemed to hold it," Walter said. "We just need to chain it again." He kept his flashlight and attention on the knight, watching for any slight movement.

"Do we chain him up in here?" Sadie asked.

"I don't know," Angus told her. "We'll have to see what ideas Quinn has."

"I hope he gets here soon," Laura said. "That knight gives me the heebie-jeebies."

"He'll be here soon," Walter assured her.

Jackson, Quinn, and several of his men arrived just a few minutes later. They inspected the secret door with wide eyes.

"I never knew this was here," he told them. His men agreed with him.

"The knight is in here," Angus said, making way for the men so they could enter the inner cell.

"Hard to believe," Quinn said. "One of your kids found the way in here?"

"Scotty did," C.J. said.

Scotty couldn't help but smile at the attention.

"Excellent work," Quinn told him. "Now we have to do our part."

He sent one man for some chains and another for a cart.

"We'll chain it up and move it out of here to a more secure location," he told the others.

Once the men returned, they gingerly took the sword from the knight and maneuvered it face down onto the metal cart. Wrapping the chains around the knight and through the metal bars of the cart, they pulled them as tight as they could and secured them with heavy padlocks.

"Hopefully, that will hold it," Quinn said.

"Do you have someplace secure that has more light than down here?" Angus asked. "We need to examine it closer."

"If you need light," Quinn said, "we'll have to take it upstairs. We don't have electricity down here, so the only light would be torches."

"Is there somewhere upstairs that we can lock it up?" Walter asked.

Quinn thought for a moment. "I think there is a spot where we can contain it." He directed his men to take the cart down the hall and up the stairs.

Once they were on the main level, the group followed him outside, dragging the cart behind them.

He headed to the western gate of the castle. Once the cart with the knight was inside the gate, he instructed the men to drop the portcullis.

"Once we close the inside portcullis, there will be no way that it can force its way out of here," Quinn told them. "It can only get out if we let it out."

"We need to examine it," Angus said. "Walter and I will do that. Everyone else should go outside when the portcullis is closed."

"We need to turn it over," Walter said. "Quinn, could a couple of your men help us with that?"

"Bram and I will stay and help," Quinn said.

"Once we turn it over and secure it," Angus said, "you two should leave as well."

Quinn nodded.

The rest of the group moved back into the castle's inner courtyard and watched the portcullis lower into place with a heavy thud.

The four men went to work removing the locks and chains. They turned the armor over and quickly refastened the restraints, again securing the knight to the cart.

When that was done, Quinn signaled for the portcullis to be raised enough for them to leave. Angus sent the knight's sword with Quinn so that they would separate the weapon from the knight.

As Quinn and Bram exited, they lowered the grating into place again.

Angus and Walter went to work examining the armor.

They raised the visor on the helmet and shined a light inside. As they suspected, it appeared empty.

"Should we remove one gauntlet and see what happens there?" Walter asked.

"Let's do that," Angus agreed.

They tried to remove the gauntlet, but they could not. The chains across the arms prevented them from moving.

"What about a greave?" Walter suggested.

They proceeded to one leg and removed the sabaton that covered the right foot. They gingerly pulled on the piece of armor covering the shin and foot. It slid off with little effort.

They brought the metal piece over to the gate to get better light on it.

"There are definite scratches where the chains bound it," Walter said. "Metal can affect it."

Angus returned to the knight's leg and shone a light into the armor. He could see through the leg and into the space behind the breastplate.

"It's empty," Angus said.

"Not a surprise," Walter said. He peered at the leg piece again, but seeing detail in the waning light was tricky.

"We should call it a night," Walter said.

"You're right," Angus agreed.

"Maybe we can take the leg with us," Walter suggested. "I don't think it can cause much damage."

"Good idea," Angus said. "Then we can examine it in a better light." As they turned and signaled Quinn to raise the portcullis, the arm of the knight moved and slammed into the cart.

Chapter 24

"Look out!" C.J. shouted.

Angus and Walter backed away from the cart toward the gate. Everyone stared at the knight, wondering what it would do next.

After several minutes, there was no more movement from the armor. Angus cautiously approached the cart. When he reached it, he laughed.

"I must have loosened the arm when I tried to remove the gauntlet," he told the others. "The arm slipped out, and gravity took over."

"I'm ready to get out of here all the same," Walter said.

"Me too," Angus agreed.

Quinn signaled for the portcullis to be raised. With a groan of metal, the grating rose. Angus and Walter slipped out of the gatehouse as soon as they could duck under. The portcullis reversed and dropped back to the ground, locking the one-legged knight in the shadows of its new prison.

"I'll have a couple of men stand guard," Quinn told them. "They will let us know if there is any movement."

"Thank you," Angus said. "We'll take the leg and sword into the castle and continue our examination later."

Quinn showed them to a spare room with a bit of furniture. To secure the leg for the night, they placed it in a wooden box and latched it. They set the box on a table and locked the door to the room.

After securing the leg in a locked room, they retired for the night.

When Maeve, Keir, and Mollie returned early the following day, the castle staff sprang into action to prepare to meet with local dignitaries to acknowledge Keir as the new Lord MacGregor.

Quinn dispatched several men to invite the head of the local church, the mayor of Oorlich, and other town dignitaries to the castle.

"Is Keir officially the new Lord?" Angus asked Maeve once there was a lull in the activity.

"Yes," she said, "now we just need to meet with certain officials so that they can acknowledge his claim."

"Could they doubt it?"

"They could, but it would just drag things out, and we would have to present evidence for his claim."

"Evidence?" Walter asked.

"Birth certificate to prove he is Alastair's son," she told him. "But I don't think anyone will claim he isn't."

"What happens now?" Walter asked.

"We wait," Maeve told him. "Let's go into the study. We'll meet with them there."

Keir and Molly were already in the study waiting with Quinn when the rest entered the room. Keir was sitting in a chair near the fireplace while they had moved the other chairs out of the way.

"What do I do?" Keir asked his mother.

"You don't need to do anything but nod to everyone when they greet you as Lord MacGregor," his mother instructed him. "I will do most of the talking."

The Young Explorers and their parents sat in the chairs out of the way and prepared to observe what would happen.

When all was ready, Quinn left the study to wait for the visitors.

Everybody waited in the study in silence. Keir sat in the chair, his legs pulled up and his arms wrapped around them. Maeve stood by Mollie with her arm around the girl.

When the guests arrived, Maeve had Mollie stand behind Keir's chair just to his left. She had Keir sit straight with his hands folded in his lap. Once they were ready, she had Quinn let them in.

As each entered the study, they greeted Keir, then his mother, and took a step back to wait for the rest of the visitors.

Once everyone was there, Maeve began.

"Thank you for coming today. We have just returned from the House of Lords. They have heard Keir's claim to Alastair MacGregor's title and certified that claim. Keir MacGregor is the new Lord of MacGregor castle."

The visitors all nodded at the news. One man stepped forward and bowed to Keir.

"As Mayor of Oorlich," the man said, "Let me be the first to congratulate you on your lordship."

One by one, the others introduced themselves and added their congratulations. To each one, Keir nodded his acknowledgment.

When they were done, Maeve spoke again, "As Lord MacGregor is a minor, I will act as executor of the estate until he comes of age."

"Of course," the mayor said.

The others mumbled their agreement.

"Thank you for coming today," Maeve told them. "I'm sure we will meet individually in the coming days to discuss any concerns."

"Naturally," the mayor agreed.

One by one, they bowed again to Keir, repeated their congratulations, and left the castle.

When they were gone, Keir seemed to relax.

"You did well," Maeve told him. "You're done for now."

Quinn and the rest of the adults restored the furniture to their regular places.

"Keir really is Lord MacGregor now?" C.J. asked his father.

"Yes, he is," Angus said.

"Do you feel different?" C.J. asked Keir.

"Not really," he said, pulling his legs up again. "But I'm scared."

There was the sound of someone running out in the front hall. A man pushed into the study. He was out of breath.

"What is it?" Quinn asked.

"The knight," he said, trying to catch his breath. "It's moving."

Quinn followed the man back outside.

Angus and Walter looked at each other and ran to the room where they had locked the knight's leg. C.J. and Sadie followed them.

They could hear thumping inside when they reached the room door. They quickly unlocked the door and opened it.

The box containing the leg was still on the table, but a thumping sound was coming from within.

When they opened the box, they stared at the leg with fascination and horror.

C.J. and Sadie looked at the inside of the box for just a moment before their parents slammed the lid on it, hustled them out of the room, and locked the door.

They looked at each other in disbelief. They saw the leg flopping around inside the box, kicking at the sides furiously.

Chapter 25

They found the knight struggling with the chains when they joined the others outside the gatehouse. But the chains held fast.

"Do you think he can break them?" C.J. asked his father.

"They look like they're holding right now," Angus told him. "But who knows how long they will last?"

The knight thrashed about under the chains, causing the metal cart to rock back and forth. It made no noise except for the clatter of the armor, cart, and chains.

"Even if it gets loose from the cart," Quinn said, "There is no way it can get through the grating."

"I hope not," Walter said.

"If it did," Angus said, "what could we do about it?"

No one had an answer for him.

They all watched it with morbid fascination as it continued to test its bonds.

"I think the kids should return to the castle," Edna said. "This is too much, even for me."

"You're right," Teresa told her.

"Let's all go back inside," Angus said. "We'll leave Quinn and his men to watch over the knight."

Despite the kids' protests, they all filed back into the castle and returned to the study to discuss their options to neutralize the knight.

"As far as I can tell," Angus began, "we have two choices."

"Destroy the armor?" C.J. blurted out.

"Yes," Angus said. "One option is to find out how to destroy enough of the armor to make it harmless."

"How do we do that?" Sadie asked.

"That is a good question," Angus said.

"The chains caused some dents in it," Walter said. "We saw those the first time we examined it."

"Maybe we could pound it flat so it couldn't move," Scotty suggested.

"That is a distinct possibility," His father told him.

"Can we burn it?" Laura asked.

"It would have to be extremely hot to melt that kind of metal," Teresa said.

"We could bury it again," C.J. said.

"Yes, it worked the last time," Angus agreed. "But it also means someone can re-release it as we did."

"We need to find a more permanent solution," Jackson said.

"I agree," Edna said. "We need to take care of it once and for all."

"What other options do we have?" Angus asked.

"We can try to remove the curse," Sadie suggested.

"Do we know anything about removing curses?" Teresa asked.

"Most theories I've read say that only the person who created the curse can remove it," Laura said.

"And she's long gone," C.J. said.

"Can a different witch remove the curse of another witch?" Sadie asked.

"Possibly," Laura said. "If she knows the curse. But what other witch do we know?"

"What about that old woman who went after Keir's dad?" Sadie asked.

"What? Morag?" Angus asked. "Is she a witch?"

"She's related to the witch. Maybe she's one, too."

"Maybe."

"She doesn't seem like she would want to remove the curse," Edna said. "It's more likely she wants to keep it."

"Alastair tried to get her to give up her hate," Angus said, "but she had no interest in doing that."

"Maybe Greer could talk her into it," C.J. said.

"She probably carries the same hate as her grandmother," Edna said. "After all, she was the one that hid the knight in the dungeon."

"That's right," Teresa said. "She's been breaking into the castle. She's probably been trying to find the knight."

"No," Angus said. "Trying to get Morag to remove the curse isn't the best use of our time."

"Do we have any other options?" Walter asked. He looked around the room at everyone's faces. No one had any additional ideas.

"That means we must figure out how to destroy the armor," Angus said.

"We can pound it with hammers or torch it," Jackson said.

Angus smiled. "That's a simplified version of the problem," he said. "But I think we need some more powerful options."

"How do we know hammers won't work?" C.J. asked.

Angus looked at his son for a moment. "I guess we don't know for sure."

"How do we find out without risking our lives with the knight?" Edna asked.

"We have the leg," C.J. said.

"Yes, we do," Angus agreed. "We can test our theories on the leg, and if it is successful, we can go after the knight."

"Let's do it," Walter said.

While Jackson went to get Quinn, the rest went to see what the leg was up to. When they reached the room, they could still hear the familiar thumping.

Inside the latched box, the leg sounded like it was still active.

They waited for Quinn and Jackson to return before they opened the box.

When they returned, they brought hammers, sledges, and large pliers.

They passed out the tools and prepared to take on the leg. Those with pliers stood at the ready. When Angus opened the box lid, they each tried to grab a piece of the armor and hold it in place.

The armor was strong, but they immobilized it enough to try the hammers.

Walter took one of the heavier hammers and picked a spot on the armor, away from the various pliers holding it. The hammer came down on the leg with a clang. He hit it again and again. After several blows, they realized it did little more than scuff the metal.

"Let's try the sledge," Quinn said. He signaled for one of his men to use the sledge on the armor.

As the man raised the sledge, several people holding the armor with the pliers voiced their concern.

"Don't worry," Quinn told them. "He has great aim."

As he raised the sledge again, everyone leaned away as far as they could. The sledge came down with a bang. The box and table trembled under the blow.

He hit it once more and then one time after that. When he put the sledge down, everyone peered into the box. There wasn't even a dent in the leg armor.

Chapter 26

"Well," Angus said. "That didn't work."

When everyone let go of the leg, Angus slammed the lid back down on the box and latched it again. The thumping resumed.

"Anyone have any more ideas?" Walter asked.

"Anyone have torches?" Jackson said. No one laughed at his joke.

"We don't have torches," Quinn said. "But there is a smithy in town."

"A blacksmith made the armor," Angus said. "Maybe a blacksmith can unmake it."

"It's worth a try," Walter said.

Walter and Jackson grabbed the ends of the box and followed the rest of the group out of the castle and into the town.

The blacksmith was in the middle of his supper when the crowd knocked on his door.

"What do ye want?" the man asked Quinn, the only man he recognized.

"Graeme, we have a problem that you might solve," Quinn told him.

"What's that?"

"Let's go into your shop."

They went into the building behind his house. Shelves, tools, and pieces of metal lined the walls. In the center was an anvil mounted on a large block of wood. At the back of the shop was a massive brick forge.

They placed the box on the anvil. He stared at it.

"What kind of animal do ye have in there?"

"It's not an animal," Quinn told him.

"What is it then?" Graeme asked.

Quinn nodded to Walter and Jackson. They unlatched the box and flipped open the lid.

"Saints preserve us," the man exclaimed, falling away from the box.

"The saints won't help us with this," Quinn told him. "But we hope you can."

"What do you think I can do with that?" he asked.

"Can you melt it down in your forge?"

"But it's moving."

"Hopefully, it will stop once it's melted."

He stared at the leg bouncing around inside the box.

"Close that thing up," he told them.

"You won't help us?" Quinn asked.

"It'll take the fires of hell to get rid of that thing," Graeme said. "I'll have to fire up the forge as hot as possible."

The man set to work throwing several lumps of coal into the bottom of the forge and using bellows to feed the fire more oxygen.

They all could feel the heat radiate out against their faces and hands. Although the sweat soon began, they were glad to have the protection of their clothes against the output of the forge.

After a while, Graeme seemed to be happy with the fire level. He grabbed a giant pair of metal tongs and returned to the box.

"Open the box," he commanded. Jackson and Walter opened it again.

He reached the tongs in and, after several attempts, he got a grip on the armor. He pulled it out of the box but almost lost his balance when he turned to put it in the forge.

"This thing is strong," he said as he regained his footing and pushed the armor into the fire.

There was a screeching sound as the armor entered the fire, as if crying out in pain.

"Was that real?" C.J. asked.

"Probably just the metal expanding with the heat," the blacksmith said. C.J. wasn't sure he was right.

The armor continued to move about inside the forge and kicked some embers out at the onlookers and onto the floor.

Soon, the armor was bright red.

"Stand back, everyone," he called. He grabbed a heavy hammer with one hand and the tongs in the other. Plunging the tongs back into the fire pit, he pulled the glowing armor out and slammed it down on the anvil.

The room rang with the sound of the blows from the hammer raining down on the super-heated metal.

Heat and exertion caused sweat to pour off the blacksmith as he tried to flatten the armor.

After what seemed like an hour to the onlookers, but was only about 10 minutes, Graeme stopped his assault on the piece of metal. It had cooled enough that the glow had almost entirely disappeared.

Everyone peered close at the armor. It had not changed a bit. And it was still squirming around in the smith's tongs.

He plunged it into a bucket of water nearby. It hissed as the metal cooled, and a cloud of steam rose above the bucket.

Angus reopened the wooden box just as Graeme turned to drop it in. They closed the lid and threw the latch again.

The blacksmith breathed heavily and sighed. "I've seen nothing like it," he said. "Can't even dent it. It would take far more force than I can apply, probably tons of it."

"I can't say we're not disappointed," Angus said. "But we appreciate you trying."

Quinn paid the blacksmith for his efforts, and they left him to go back to his supper.

When they returned to the castle, they checked on the knight in the gatehouse. It surprised them that his other leg had come off in its struggles.

"Is anyone good with a rope?" Walter asked.

"You want us to lasso that other leg?" Quinn asked.

"If we separate him from both his legs," Walter said, "He won't get very far if he breaks free."

"Ross there grew up on a sheep farm," Quinn said, pointing out a young man in his late teens. "Can you lasso it, lad?" he asked the teen.

"Sure can," Ross said.

They fetched him a rope and a second box to store the leg. He quickly put together a lasso. He stood beside the grating and slipped the rope and his arms through.

After preparing for the throw, he let the rope fly. It landed just short of the armor. It was just as active as the one in the box.

"Hard to get a good throw through this thing," he said, pointing at the portcullis. "But I'll get it."

The rope landed on the leg on his second try, but it hopped out before he could tug it tight.

"Third time's the charm," he said, and it was. The rope encircled the leg, and he snagged it. He dragged it to the fence, and they carefully fished the flopping piece of metal through the grating.

"Well done, Ross," Quinn told him.

They dropped the leg in the other box and latched it closed.

"Now, let's lock these away with the sword," Quinn said.

"Maybe we should lock them in three different places to separate them," Angus suggested. "We don't want someone breaking in and getting all three of them."

Quinn showed them to three different rooms, and after locking up one item in each, he placed a guard at all three doors.

"What do we do now?" C.J. asked his dad.

"I don't know. But that's a problem for tomorrow."

Chapter 27

The conversation quickly turned to their next steps with the knight when they gathered for breakfast the following day.

"We can't seem to destroy the armor," Angus said. "What does that leave us for options?"

"Removing the curse," C.J. said.

"Can you do that?" Keir asked.

"We're not sure," Angus told him.

Keir glanced at his mother.

"We're going to try," he told the boy.

"We need to talk to Morag," Laura said. "If anyone knows how to remove the curse, she would."

"Do we know where she lives?" Angus asked.

"I do," C.J. said. "I met her outside her house the first time we went into the village. She wasn't too friendly."

"I believe it," his dad said. "Still, I think I should go talk to her."

"Can we come too?" C.J. asked.

"I think we should keep it to just a couple of us," Edna said. "We don't want to make her too defensive."

"Yes," Angus agreed. "I think Walter and Edna should go. They have MacGregor family connections."

"I agree," Edna said.

"Do you think she can remove the curse?" Maeve asked.

"We don't know," Angus said. "I hope so. Step one is finding out if she can. Step two is getting her to do it."

"Do you think you can convince her?" Maeve asked.

"We have to," Edna said. "We don't know what else we can do."

She saw Keir was on the verge of tears. She kneeled by his chair. "We will get rid of the knight, ok?" she said to him.

He nodded.

"When should we go?" Walter asked.

"I think we should go as soon as possible," Edna said. "The sooner we go...."

The door burst open, interrupting her, and a guard rushed in.

"What is it?" Quinn asked.

"It's gone," the man said. "The box was open, and it was gone."

Quinn jumped up and hurried out with the man. Angus and the kids chased them. The rest of the adults stayed with Keir and his family.

When they reached the room, the door was open. The box had fallen off the table and was lying open on its side. There was no sign of the leg armor.

"What happened?" Quinn asked him.

"I heard a crash in the room, so I unlocked the door to check. I found the box just as it is."

"Did you search the room?"

"I looked around, but I didn't see it anywhere. Then I came to get you," he said.

"Search again," Quinn commanded.

Angus and the kids spread out in the room to search. They looked under and behind the furniture. And they checked the locks on the windows.

"No one came in or out through the windows," Angus said.

"And it is not in the room," Quinn added.

"We need to check the other pieces," Angus said.

They rushed to the room where they had locked the other leg piece. The guard was sitting in a chair by the door.

"Have you heard anything from the room?" Quinn asked him.

"I could hear the armor thumping around in the box, but that died off in the middle of the night," he told them.

"Open the door," Quinn said.

As soon as the door was open, they rushed in. The box was still on the table. Angus examined the box.

"The latch is open," he said.

He lifted the lid and glanced inside. It was empty.

"It must still be in here," Quinn said.

They spread out again.

They turned every piece of furniture over and even pulled the cushions from a sofa.

"What's that?" C.J. said, pointing at a lump in a rug by the door.

The leg popped out from under the rug and rolled to the door.

"Get it," Quinn shouted.

The leg was faster than they imagined. It hooked the foot piece on the door and pulled it shut, slipping out as it slammed.

Angus was the first to reach the door and pulled it open. There was no sign of the leg in the hallway.

"Where could it have gone?" Quinn asked.

"It could be almost anywhere as fast as it was," Angus said.

There was a crash and the sound of glass breaking nearby.

"Was that the sword?" Quinn asked, and everyone followed him into the hallway and to the room where they locked the weapon.

The guard at that door already had the key in the lock and opened it just as they arrived.

When they entered the room, the sword was not where they had left it. Angus ran to the window. A break in the pane was less than a foot wide and a few inches tall.

"What do you see?" Quinn demanded, hurrying to the window.

"There's glass outside," Angus said. "Whatever broke the glass was breaking out, not in."

Quinn stepped up next to him. "My God," he said.

The sword was sliding along the ground toward the outer wall.

"Is the gatehouse that way?" Angus asked.

"Yes, it is," Quinn said. "Let's get out there."

They returned to the front hall, where they met Walter and Jackson.

"Did you find it?" Walter asked.

"No," Angus told him without slowing down. "But we know where it is going."

They crossed the front hall and ran out into the courtyard. The gatehouse was just around the corner from the main doors to the castle, and it only took a minute or two to cross the yard and get to it.

When they arrived, they found the two guards standing and staring into the shadows of the gate.

"Did you see the sword?" Quinn asked them.

They could only nod dumbly.

"Where is it?" Quinn demanded.

One guard pointed into the gatehouse. When their eyes adjusted to the dimness, they saw the knight standing on both legs, holding its sword at the ready.

Chapter 28

"When did it get loose?" Quinn asked the guards.

"I don't know," one guard told him. "It kept struggling well into the night, but it got so dark, we couldn't see it."

"In the middle of the night, it stopped struggling," the other guard said. "We heard nothing from it afterward."

"It must have gotten loose then," Quinn said. "It was probably waiting for the legs and sword to escape."

"We can't secure it with the chains anymore," Angus said. "I don't think anyone should go in there."

"Or risk letting it out," Quinn said.

Quinn assigned two different guards to watch over the knight for the day.

"Let me know immediately if anything changes," he told them. "And don't go near the grating."

They left the guards there and returned to the keep.

When they joined the others, Maeve was the first to speak.

"What happened?" she asked Quinn.

"The knight broke free of the chains and is in one piece again," he told her.

Keir grew pale, and his eyes widened.

"It's still trapped in the gatehouse," Quinn reassured him. "That should hold it until we figure out what to do."

"It will not stop until I'm dead," Keir said softly.

"We won't let that happen," Maeve said.

"It came after my dad, and we couldn't stop it."

"We're prepared now," Quinn told him.

"I'm scared," Keir said.

Mollie nodded, "So am I."

"We all are," Maeve said. "But to defeat this curse, we must try to stand up to it."

"How?" Keir said.

"We need to get the curse removed," C.J. said.

"How do we do that?"

"We don't know how," Angus said. "But we know who."

"Who?"

"We need to speak with a woman from town. Someone who may know exactly how to remove the curse," Angus said.

"Are you going to talk to her soon?" Keir asked.

"Walter and I need to talk about what we are going to say to her," Edna told him. "We will go see her in the morning."

"I hope I last that long," Keir said.

"We'll keep you safe until we can get rid of the curse," Quinn said.

"Don't you worry so," Maeve said. "Mollie and I are here. So is Quinn."

"And we are here for you, too," Edna said.

Sadie chimed in. "Even..."

"Greer!" C.J. shouted, pointing at the window.

They saw Greer's face looking in at them.

Quinn rushed out of the room. He called to several of his men as he crossed the front hall to the main doors.

The four kids were following close on their heels.

The girl ran across the courtyard as they exited the castle. She was almost to the gatehouse and off the castle grounds when a couple of guards at that gate grabbed her arms. She nearly wrenched free but could not break their grip.

They held her until Quinn and the others could confront her.

"What are you doing here?" Quinn asked. "You are not welcome in the castle."

"You obviously can't keep me out," she told him.

"Were you trying to release the knight?"

"Does it look like it?"

"I will let you go tonight," Quinn told her. "But if we find you on the grounds again, we will have you arrested for trespassing."

"Am I supposed to be scared?" she asked.

"Yes," Quinn said. "Jail is no laughing matter."

"You can try to have me arrested," the girl said.

"Oh, I will," he said, motioning to the guards. "Take her out."

She began struggling against the guards. It took everything they had to keep her under control.

Quinn waved a couple more guards over to help. Grabbing her legs, they carried her through the gatehouse to the drawbridge.

They almost dropped her at one point but kept a hold of her.

Carrying her out of the gatehouse, they continued straight across the drawbridge. It wasn't until they were on the road leading to town that they finally let her down onto her own two feet.

"Now go home," Quinn told her. "And don't come back here."

She stood in the middle of the road, scowling at Quinn and his men.

"You think you've won?" She asked.

"There's no winning this game," he said. "For either of us."

She continued to stare him down, and after several minutes of silence, she turned and stomped down the road away from the castle.

They stood there until she disappeared down the road and were sure she was gone. Slowly, they returned to the castle.

When they entered the courtyard, the guards at the other gatehouse hailed them. They were waving frantically.

They ran over to them to see what the commotion was about. The men seemed almost hysterical.

"I don't know what happened," one of them said.

"We were just standing here," the other said. "Minding our own business."

"Still standing guard, of course," the first corrected him.

"Yes, naturally, we were standing guard. One moment he was here," the second started.

"And the next he wasn't," the first finished.

"Who wasn't?" Quinn demanded.

"That's what we're trying to tell you," the first guard said.

"He wasn't," the second said, pointing into the dark gatehouse.

"Give me your torch," Quinn said. The first guard handed him his flashlight.

Quinn pointed the light into the darkness and waved it around until he could see every corner of the gatehouse.

"I don't believe it," Quinn said.

"What?" Angus asked.

"The knight isn't here," Quinn said, handing the flashlight to Angus.

Angus searched every corner of the gatehouse and even around the ceiling, trying to find where the knight could have gone.

There were no exits in the gatehouse except through the grating where the guards stood.

"The knight," Angus said. "It's gone."

Chapter 29

Keir was talking to his mother and sister when C.J. and the others burst into the room.

"The knight is gone!" C.J. shouted.

"What?" Maeve asked. "I thought you said it couldn't escape the gatehouse."

"I don't know how it escaped," Quinn told her. "But it did. We must move Keir to somewhere safer."

"Go with Quinn," Maeve told him. "You too, Mollie." Both of her kids followed Quinn and his men out of the room.

"Can we go with them?" C.J. asked.

"No," Maeve told him. "You can visit them later."

"Why don't you go to your rooms," Angus said. "Until we find out where the knight went this time, no one is safe."

They reluctantly went upstairs to C.J.'s room. None of them wanted to go to their rooms alone.

"Could it have gone back to the dungeon?" Scotty asked, looking out the window at the courtyard below.

"I'm sure they will check there," Sadie said.

"Where else could it have gone?" Laura asked.

"Who knows?" C.J. said.

"She might," Scotty said, pointing out the window.

The others looked out toward the town. Greer was walking away from the castle into town.

"I thought she left when they kicked her out," Sadie said.

"She probably let the knight out," C.J. said. "We should go find out what she knows."

The others agreed, so they left C.J.'s room and hurried out of the castle. They couldn't see Greer anywhere when they reached the road into town.

"She'll probably be at Morag's place," C.J. said. "This way!"

They followed him toward the center of town. As they approached the grandmother's house, they spotted Greer coming from the opposite direction.

They ran toward her, but she saw them before they could get close. She ran back the way she had come. They pursued her through the streets.

She paused at a corner to look back and see if they were still on her tail. When she saw they were following, she turned the corner and disappeared down a side street.

C.J. and Scotty ran to the corner to catch up to her. Sadie grabbed Laura's arm and pulled her down a different side street.

When C.J. and Scotty turned the corner, they could see Greer ahead. She again paused at an intersection, almost like she was waiting for them. After a moment, she plunged around the corner to the right and out of sight.

C.J. was tiring. But he and Scotty kept going. When they looked around that corner, she was almost at the end of that block.

Looking back at C.J. and Scotty, she wasn't looking where she was going and ran headlong into Sadie and Laura, who appeared from around the corner behind her.

She tripped and fell, rolling onto the pavement. The four kids quickly surrounded her.

She got to her feet and stared at her adversaries.

"Did you let the knight loose?" C.J. asked her.

"What?" Greer said.

"Did you let the knight loose?" Sadie repeated.

"It got loose?"

"You know it did," Scotty said.

"Why do you think I had anything to do with that?"

"Because you've been helping it ever since we found it," C.J. said.

Greer said nothing. She glanced around the circle of kids, looking for a way out.

"You may as well admit it," Sadie told her. "You and your grandmother want the MacGregors to die."

"That doesn't mean I let it out," she said. "It was there when your minions threw me out of the castle."

"It was already gone by then," C.J. said.

"You can't prove I let it out," Greer said. "Even if I did, so what?"

"You're responsible for Lord MacGregor's death," Sadie said. "That makes you a murderer."

"I didn't kill him," Greer said.

"Not with your own hands," C.J. said. "But you aided the knight."

Greer shrugged and moved to dart through their circle, but they closed ranks to prevent her from getting through.

"We should turn you over to the police," Laura said.

"And tell them what?" Greer said. "That I made a suit of armor kill someone? They'll laugh at you."

"We know you did," Sadie said.

"You know it," Greer said. "And I know it. But no one is going to believe you."

"You admit it?" C.J. asked.

"Why not," Greer said. "The MacGregors killed our kin, so why shouldn't I help her kill them from the grave?"

"Because one MacGregor killed your kin," C.J. said. "Not all of them."

"It's their family against mine," Greer told him.

"The MacGregors are not against your family," Sadie said. "I'm a MacGregor, but I'm not against you."

"Doesn't matter," Greer said. "The knight will kill all the Lords."

"Keir has done nothing against you or your grandmother," Scotty said.

"And you're helping the knight kill him," Laura said.

"I'm sorry about that," Greer said. "I am. He is a nice kid."

"Why should he die then?" C.J. asked.

"I wish it could be different, but he is a MacGregor lord."

"You won't help him?" Sadie asked. "He's just a boy."

"I wish I could," she said. "But I can't."

"You can help us save him," C.J. said.

"No, I can't. The curse has sealed his fate. There is nothing I can do about it."

"Nothing you can do, or nothing you will do."

"Doesn't matter," Greer said. "She cursed the MacGregors. I can't do anything about that, and even if I could, I wouldn't."

C.J. was about to say something more, but Greer twisted around and rushed at him. She rammed into him, causing him to stumble backward and fall to the ground. Before anyone could react, she disappeared down the street and into the darkness.

Sadie helped C.J. to his feet.

"Should we go after her?" she asked.

"No," C.J. said. "We need to find another way."

"We need to talk to her grandmother," Laura said.

Chapter 30

They came down for breakfast late the following day to find their parents had already eaten.

"Slept in, did you?" Angus asked.

"We were up late," C.J. admitted.

"Doing what?" Edna asked.

C.J. told them about confronting Greer in town the night before and what she told them.

"You shouldn't have done that," Teresa said. "You don't know what she might have done."

"We found out she won't help us," C.J. said.

"Walter and I will try to meet with Morag and see what she has to say," Edna said.

"She'll be as stubborn as Greer," Sadie said.

"Maybe, but we have to try," Edna told her. "C.J., can you tell us where she lives?"

"I can show you," C.J. said.

"No," Walter said. "I think you have done enough for the moment. Just tell us."

C.J. gave them directions to her house. Edna and Walter excused themselves and headed down to the village.

They didn't take long to follow C.J.'s instructions and find the little house. They pushed open the small gate and knocked on the door.

There was no response from within and no sign that the old woman was home.

"Morag," Walter called, knocking on the door again.

There was still no answer.

"Maybe she's not here," Edna said.

"I think she's in there," Walter said, then knocked on the door again. "Morag, I know you're in there."

After a few moments of silence, they heard a low voice. "Leave me be."

"We would like to speak with you about Greer," Walter said.

"What about her?" Morag asked.

"Please let us in," Edna said. "We don't want to shout it to everyone on the street."

The old woman inside was silent again.

Edna looked at Walter. He shrugged. They were about to knock again when they heard a click, and the door opened.

Walter stepped into the dimness of the old house, with Edna just behind him. When their eyes adjusted to the darkness of the house, they found a stark room with just a few pieces of furniture. A fireplace, dark and cold, stood at the end of the room.

The old woman stood by a door leading to the back of the house with a chair between her and them.

"My name is Walter," Walter introduced himself, "and this is my wife, Edna."

"I know who ye are," Morag said. "You are kin of the MacGregors."

"Yes," Edna said.

"You have something to say about my granddaughter?" Morag asked.

"We want you to help your granddaughter," Edna told her.

"Why? Is she in some trouble?"

"Yes, and she will be in more trouble soon if you don't help her."

"What kind of trouble?" Morag asked.

"She hid the knight after we found it," Walter said, "And became an accessory in Alastair MacGregor's death."

"The knight did that, not her," Morag laughed.

"She's also been helping the knight to escape," Edna said. "If the knight kills Keir MacGregor, his blood will be on her, too."

"No, their blood is on Gavin MacGregor."

"Keir is just a little boy. He's done nothing to you and your family."

"The boy is a MacGregor."

"He is innocent," Walter said. "Gavin may have killed your ancestor, but Keir had nothing to do with that."

"What does that have to do with Greer?" Morag asked.

"We ask that you remove the curse before any more bloodshed," Edna said. "Before anything happens to Keir and before Greer has any more blood on her hands."

"We want nothing to happen to Greer," Walter said.

"What would happen to her?" Morag asked.

"She's helped the knight," Edna said. "They could arrest her."

"And send her to jail," Walter said.

"They wouldn't do that," Morag said. "They have no evidence."

"Many at the castle have seen her sneaking inside the castle and helping the knight," Walter said.

"You don't want her to go to jail, do you?" Edna asked.

Morag frowned and paced back and forth.

"Do you want her to go to jail?" Walter asked.

"No," she snapped and turned on them. Then she sighed. "What can I do about it?"

"If you help remove the curse," Edna said. "The knight can't do any more damage, and Greer can't get into any more trouble."

"Do you want Greer to get into trouble?" Walter asked.

"Of course not," Morag shouted. She began pacing once again.

Walter looked at Edna. Edna smiled at him, and Walter turned back to the old woman.

"If you remove the curse," he told her, "these troubles go away."

"You wouldn't try to punish her?" Morag asked.

"No," Edna said. "We just want the curse removed so the knight won't harm anyone else."

"I don't know," the old woman said.

"Please, Morag," Walter said. "It will be best for everyone, including you and Greer."

"We can help you any way we can," Edna said. "All you have to do is tell us what you need from us."

Morag turned away from them and hung her head.

Edna looked at Walter and frowned at him.

"Are you ok?" Edna asked her.

The old woman put her hands to her face, and they could hear her sniffling.

"There is no reason to be sad," Edna said. "Help us put this curse behind us, and everything will be all right."

Morag continued to stand with her back to them. Her shoulders trembled.

"You asked what I need you to do," she said in a voice barely audible.

"We will do anything you need us to," Edna repeated.

She spun around with a frightening smile on her face. They realized she hadn't been sobbing but laughing instead.

"What I need you to do is get out of my house."

They stood in shock, staring at the diminutive woman.

When they didn't move, she grabbed a nearby cane and shook it at them.

"I said, get out of my house," she shouted. "Now."

They retreated to the door and backed out as she advanced with the cane.

"I will never remove the curse," she said as she slammed the door in their faces.

Chapter 31

When Walter and Edna returned to the castle, they found everyone waiting for them.

"Will she remove the curse?" Sadie asked.

Edna shook her head. "She won't do it."

"There's no changing her mind?" Maeve asked.

"No," Walter said. "She is one stubborn woman."

"So where does that leave us?" C.J. asked.

"We must figure out some other way to remove the curse," Angus said. "Although I'm at a loss on how to do that."

Teresa looked at her daughter. "Laura, do you have any ideas?"

"No," she said, "I can try to do some research tomorrow."

"Can we go see Keir and Mollie tonight?" C.J. asked.

"Possibly," Maeve said. "Quinn will have to take you."

"They're not in their rooms?" Sadie asked.

"No, they are in a safe room in a secret area of the castle."

"Cool," C.J. said.

"You'll have to keep it a secret," Maeve told him. "Don't tell anyone how to get there, and never go there alone."

"We will," C.J. said. "I mean, we won't. Uh, I mean, we will keep it a secret and won't tell anyone."

Maeve smiled at him. "I knew what you meant. I'll have Quinn take you."

"Can we all go?" Sadie asked.

"Of course," Maeve said. "I'm sure they both would love the company."

They all followed Quinn to the door.

"You'll have to stay quiet as we make our way through the castle." He told them. "We don't want to attract attention to ourselves."

They all nodded their understanding.

He led them out into the front hall and down several passageways to a small door at the base of one of the round towers.

Inside was a stairway that curved up around the inside of the tower. They followed the stairs up several levels, then through another small door into a hallway.

He paused and held his hand out to stop them. He listened intently for a moment, then continued down the corridor, waving them on.

The hall opened to a balcony overlooking a large space. He motioned for them to stay close to the wall and away from the railing.

He led them around two sides of the room and down another hallway.

After passing several regular-sized doors, he stopped at a rather large one.

"Wait here," he told them. He carefully opened the door and stepped into the room. After a moment, he returned and waved for them to go in. He closed the door behind them.

There were twelve suits of armor lining the walls of the long room: six on one side and another six facing them on the other side.

He saw their faces and smiled. "None of these are cursed. They have all been here for centuries."

He led them down the middle of the room toward a door on the other end.

C.J. watched each suit of armor carefully, looking for any sign of movement.

They reached the other end, with no knights jumping out at them.

Quinn opened the far door for them, and they filed into what appeared to be an empty room.

The only features of the room were two windows on one wall and a massive fireplace on the wall opposite the door.

"Are we meeting them here?" Sadie asked.

"No," Quinn said. "We still have a little way to go until we get to them."

"I hope we don't have to climb through the windows," Scotty said, his eyes wide.

"No," Quinn said again. "There is a way that's a little less dangerous."

"Where?" Laura asked.

Quinn went to the fireplace and pointed to a stone lion's head on the left side below the mantle. It had a metal ring in its mouth.

"This is one key," he told them. He took the ring in his fist and twisted it. The head of the lion turned a quarter of the way around. There was a metallic click.

"One key?" C.J. asked.

"Another one is over here," he said, pointing out a duplicate lion's head on the other side of the fireplace. He grabbed the ring and repeated the motion.

He then ducked into the fireplace and pressed against the back of it. The back wall swung in and to the side, revealing another room on the other side of the wall.

He waved the kids through and pressed the wall back into place. The room had an identical fireplace on that side, but the other three walls were blank; no windows or doors. A carpet covered most of the floor, but the bit of floor showed wood planks around the edges.

"It's a dead end," C.J. said.

"Is it?" Quinn said. "Appearances can be deceiving."

"The floor," Scotty said. "This is a wood floor. Most other rooms have stone floors."

"Good eye," Quinn said.

Scotty checked the planks along the wall opposite the fireplace, but none were loose or moved.

"That wall would be a little obvious," Quinn said.

All the kids searched the floor along the other two walls. It didn't take long for them to find a loose plank.

When they lifted the plank, they found a hollow with a metal bar below it. When they pulled the metal bar, part of the wall popped open.

They replaced the plank and pulled the wall open enough to get through. Quinn followed them into the next room.

Different from the previous two rooms, this room was far from dark and empty.

On one wall was a fireplace with a roaring fire. The room was well lit, with several sofas and chairs. A table with several plates of food stood off to the side. Two doors opened into other equally well-lit rooms.

"Hello?" Quinn called.

A moment later, a figure appeared at each of the other doorways.

"We found you," Sadie said.

In a moment, they hurried over to greet Keir and Mollie.

Chapter 32

Having the kids visit helped bolster the spirits of Keir and Mollie. They spent the evening playing Scotch Whist and checkers.

They also enjoyed some of the fruit, cheese, and crackers that were laid out on the side table.

"How long can you stay?" Keir asked C.J. at one point.

C.J. shrugged and looked at Quinn, who was lounging in a chair by the secret door that was not so secret inside.

"As long as you like," Quinn told them.

"Can they stay the night?" Mollie asked.

"If they like," Quinn said. "Your mother said it is up to you."

The two looked at the other four and were happy to see them all nod their assent.

They spent most of the evening playing cards while discussing life in the States versus life in Scotland.

It was the first time C.J. and his friends had been to Scotland, while Keir and Mollie had never been across the ocean. They had been across the channel to France once, but not the States.

When it was late, Quinn spoke up for the first time in hours. "You should probably get some sleep. Your parents wouldn't want you to stay up all night."

"Where's the bathroom?" Scotty asked.

"There isn't one in here," Keir said.

"No bathroom?" Scotty said, somewhat alarmed.

"It's an old castle," Quinn said. "We haven't installed bathrooms everywhere."

"What are we supposed to do?" Scotty asked.

"There are bedpans in the bedrooms," Quinn told him. When his face paled, Quinn laughed. "There is a bathroom just off the hallway. I can take a couple of you at a time out there, but we must be quiet and fast."

They all agreed to his conditions. None of them wanted to use the bedpans.

Scotty and Sadie were the first pair to head out with Quinn. The rest waited impatiently while listening for any sounds of them returning. Although no one would admit it, they also listened for dangerous sounds outside their safe room.

Before long, the door swung out again, and they returned.

The next pair, Mollie and Laura, followed Quinn through the maze of rooms. They returned several minutes later with no problems.

Finally, it was time for C.J. and Keir to make the trip.

Quinn opened the secret door and led them into the first empty room. He carefully closed the door behind them.

He repeated the steps to open the fireplace hearth door again, twisting one lion's head and then the other. Once they had all ducked through, he pulled the door closed again.

"That's it for the hidden doors," Quinn said. "Remember, we need to be quiet."

Both boys nodded. They understood.

They crossed the empty room and opened the door into the long hall. Even though they had seen the suits of armor before, seeing them again made both kids uneasy.

They cross the room quickly and quietly. Once they were in the hallway outside that room, they relaxed a little.

They went a short way down the corridor and around a corner to the bathroom. C.J. used the facilities first, and then Keir went in second.

Quinn suddenly grabbed C.J.'s shoulder. "Did you hear something?" he whispered.

"No," C.J. whispered back.

Quinn listened intently until Keir rejoined them in the corridor.

"What did you hear?" C.J. asked quietly.

"I'm not sure," Quinn said, "Probably nothing. Just nerves."

Quinn led them back along the corridor. He paused at the door to the armor hall. The door was ajar.

"Stand back," he told the boys. They moved to the wall across the corridor from the door.

Quinn pushed the door open and investigated the room. Everything seemed to be as it was. He went in and glanced behind the door. There was nothing there.

"Ok, boys," he said, waving them into the room.

They slowly stepped into the room. The suits of armor seemed even more menacing to them. They followed Quinn a short way through the room.

Then, C.J. stopped cold.

Quinn noticed him stop. "What's the matter?"

"There are thirteen knights now," C.J. said, his voice quivering.

Quinn glanced around. Sure enough, besides the six pairs of knights, one extra knight stood against one wall between the middle pairs.

Before anyone could say anything more, it turned and charged at them.

"Run," Quinn told the pair. He grabbed a halberd from the nearest suit of armor and brandished it at the charging knight.

Keir stood staring at the knight in horror. C.J. grabbed his arm and dragged him out of the room.

"Do you know which way to go?" C.J. demanded.

"This way," Keir said and started running down the corridor toward the room with the balcony. C.J. followed closely behind him.

They heard a clash of metal behind them in the room.

When they reached the balcony, they glanced back and saw the knight clomping down the corridor after them.

They saw Quinn enter the corridor after it as they turned and dashed around the large room.

Keir led them to a set of stairs, and they took the steps two at a time.

They could hear the knight descending the stairs as they ran to the next set of stairs.

Soon, C.J. found himself on the balcony above the front hall. They ran down the steps to the main level as fast as they could. The knight was already on the steps above them.

They turned toward the back of the castle when the knight vaulted the railing and landed in front of them, cutting them off.

The two of them reversed direction, just narrowly ducking under a swing of his sword.

They raced outside and across the courtyard, but the knight was gaining on them. When they got to the gatehouse, the knight was right behind C.J.

With one swipe of the knight's arm, C.J. flew against the side of the gatehouse wall and fell in a heap.

He looked up to see the knight swing his sword at Keir. The boy screamed, stumbled out of the gatehouse, and fell face down on the drawbridge. He didn't move again.

Chapter 33

"C.J., are you all right?"

C.J. slowly opened his eyes. His head was pounding, and he was lying on the ground. He looked up at his father bending over him.

"What happened?" he said, his voice cracking.

"You tell me," Angus said.

Then C.J. remembered. "Keir," he said, trying to sit up.

"They're tending to him," Angus assured him and helped him sit up against the gatehouse wall.

C.J. turned his head, wincing in pain to see where Keir fell. The knight was standing unmoving at the entrance to the gatehouse. Keir was lying outside with Quinn and Jackson kneeling next to him.

"Is he ok?" C.J. asked.

"I don't know," Angus told him.

They heard a siren start up somewhere in the town.

"That's the ambulance now," Angus said.

The sing-song of the siren grew louder, and soon they saw the ambulance speeding down the road toward the castle. It pulled up onto the drawbridge and stopped.

A pair of attendants jumped out with a stretcher and rushed to the boy. They waved Quinn and Jackson back and took over working on Keir.

"Why is the knight just standing there?" C.J. asked. "Is Keir dead?"

"He was still alive when we got out here," Angus told him. "I don't know why it's just standing there."

The attendants moved Keir to the stretcher and loaded him into the ambulance. Once the ambulance returned to town, Quinn and Jackson carefully moved back into the gatehouse, keeping their distance from the still immobile knight.

"How are you doing?" Quinn asked C.J.

"My head hurts," he said.

"We should have a doctor look at you, too."

"How is Keir?"

"I don't know. It doesn't look good," Quinn said. "Wait here. I'll get a car."

Quinn returned with a black sedan. He and Angus helped C.J. into the back seat. They drove around through the western gate.

It didn't take long to get to the hospital. The ambulance stood out in front.

Angus and Quinn helped C.J. inside, where a nurse took over and helped him into an examination room.

As the nurse and a doctor checked his injuries, C.J. saw several doctors and nurses working on another patient in a room across the hall. He got a quick look at Keir before one doctor closed the door.

They checked his head and shoulder and ended up bandaging his head. A nurse called C.J.'s dad into the room as the doctor finished.

"He should be fine," the doctor said. "There was some bleeding on the back of his head, but that has already stopped. The boy has bruises on his shoulder, but no broken bones. What happened to him?"

"He got into a fight," Angus said.

"With the boy in the other room?"

"What? No. It was someone else," Angus told him. "Does he need to stay in the hospital?"

"No," the doctor said. "Just some paperwork, and he can go home now."

Angus took care of the paperwork, and C.J. went to the waiting room to get news about Keir.

Everyone except Maeve, Mollie, and Quinn were there.

"Have you heard anything?" Angus asked.

"No, not yet," Edna said.

"Is Maeve here?"

"I am now," Maeve said as she entered the waiting room. She had her arm around her daughter.

"The doctors are still working on him," Walter told her.

"Is anyone in there with him?" Maeve asked.

"No," Edna said. "The doctors sent everyone out. Why don't you sit down over here?" She showed her to an empty chair.

"Would you like some water?" Walter asked.

Both she and Mollie shook their heads. "Quinn should be in shortly. He's parking the car."

The door to the waiting room opened. But instead of Quinn, it was Greer who entered.

Maeve's eyes narrowed. "Why are you here?"

Angus stood up. "I'll take care of this." He went over to the girl and guided her out of the room. Quinn was arriving when they met him in the hall.

"I don't think it is a good idea for you to be here," Angus told her. He could see the frown on Quinn's face and his balled-up fists.

"I'm sorry," she said. "I'm sorry."

"Sorry about what?" Quinn growled. "That he's still alive?"

Greer cowered away from Quinn. "No, not that. I don't want him to die. I don't want any of this anymore."

"It may be too late for that," Quinn said, and entered the waiting room, leaving Angus and Greer alone in the hall.

"I don't," Greer said.

"Still, it probably isn't a good time for you to be here," Angus told her, and then he went back into the waiting room.

"What did she want?" Maeve asked Angus when he returned.

"I think she may be realizing her mistakes," he said.

A doctor appeared from the hallway.

"Lady MacGregor?" he asked.

Maeve stood.

"You may see the boy now," he told her.

Maeve and Mollie followed the doctor down the hall and to his room.

When Angus sat down, he saw Greer was still outside the waiting room, watching and listening. He leaned over to Quinn and whispered something to him.

Quinn glanced at the waiting room door, and the conversation continued.

When Maeve and Mollie returned to the waiting room, Angus and Quinn greeted them. They had a quiet discussion that lasted several minutes.

In the end, Angus nodded solemnly and sat down with his head in his hands. Quinn stood back and bowed his head.

"How is Keir?" Edna asked. "Is he all right?"

Maeve looked down at Mollie at her side. Mollie buried her head in Maeve's shoulder.

"The knight's sword injured Keir severely," Maeve told them. "He lost so much blood. They tried to stop it."

Several people sobbed. Tears were in everyone's eyes.

"But it was just too much," Maeve continued. "There was nothing they could do. He didn't make it."

Chapter 34

Everyone returned to the castle, leaving Maeve and Mollie behind to take care of arrangements for Keir. Angus and the kids rode in the car with Quinn. It was a quiet trip, as everyone was deep in their thoughts.

As they crossed the drawbridge, the specter of the knight again confronted them as it stood in the doorway to the gatehouse.

"Why did it just stop?" C.J. asked, breaking the silence. "Keir was still alive."

"Maybe it knew that Keir was going to die," Sadie said. "It didn't need to do anything more."

"I was thinking about that," Angus said. "It stopped in the doorway to the gatehouse at the outer edge of the castle."

"Maybe it can't leave the castle?" Laura asked.

"Maybe the curse has a limit," Angus said.

Angus and the kids got out when Quinn stopped the car in the courtyard.

Angus ducked down to see Quinn across in the driver's seat. "We should try to close it up in the gatehouse again,"

"I agree," Quinn said. "I'll get some men after I park the car."

It wasn't long before he returned. He sent a couple of men up into the gatehouse to lower the portcullis on the courtyard side.

Once that grating was in place, he called for them to lower the outside one.

"It is standing right underneath the portcullis," Angus said. "Maybe we'll be lucky, and the grating will crush it."

Quinn nodded and yelled to the men to drop the grate.

They heard the latches release on the chains and saw the gate fall.

Just when it seemed it would come down right on top of the knight, it took a step backward, and the portcullis slammed into the ground in front of it. The knight did not make any other movements.

"Well," Angus said. "At least we trapped it again."

They left the knight in the gatehouse, guarded by two more guards.

"Does that mean Mollie is the new lord?" Sadie asked.

"What?" Quinn asked.

"Mollie," she repeated. "Is she the new lord?"

"I guess so," Quinn said. "Technically, she would be Lady MacGregor, but she would have the title."

"When will they go back to the House of Lords?" C.J. asked.

"I don't know," Quinn said. "Not for a few days, I suppose."

"Is there somewhere else she can hide?" Sadie said. "The knight knows about the secret rooms."

"I'll have to discuss it with Lady MacGregor," Quinn said.

They joined the others already gathered in the study.

"What happens if the knight kills Mollie too?" Laura asked.

"Lady MacGregor probably will inherit the title," Quinn said. "Or it may pass to another relative."

"You mean Dad might become a lord?" Sadie asked.

"I don't know the exact lineage," Quinn said. "If he is next in line, then yes."

"Let's just concentrate on keeping Mollie alive," Walter said, shutting down that line of discussion.

"If the knight can't leave the castle," C.J. said, "she shouldn't come back here."

"She should be safe enough for the moment," Quinn said. "She doesn't have the title yet."

"Do they have another place to live other than the castle?" Sadie asked. "I've heard royalty have several castles."

"The King does," Quinn told her, smiling, "but the MacGregors are not part of the Royal Family. This is their only home."

"But she's in danger if she stays in the castle," Sadie insisted.

"We'll figure out how to keep her safe," Angus told her.

"We couldn't keep Keir safe," Sadie said, stomping out of the room. The other three kids followed her.

They wandered around the castle and found themselves by a familiar door before long. They went into the library and sat down.

"Why don't they listen to me?" Sadie asked. "Mollie is in danger as long as she is in the castle."

"Yeah, they don't seem worried at all," Scotty said.

"Maybe they are just still in shock," C.J. said. "Tomorrow, they'll understand the danger."

Sadie sat and sulked in silence. Everyone settled into their thoughts and let her sit undisturbed for a while.

"If they won't do anything," Sadie said, breaking the silence. "We are on our own to do it ourselves."

"Do what?" Scotty asked.

"I don't know. But we must do something."

"What can we do?" Laura asked.

"We need to remove the curse," Sadie said. "That seems to be the only option."

Scotty shrugged. "But we don't know how?"

Sadie waved to the surrounding shelves. "There must be a book somewhere telling us how to do it."

"I've searched this library," Laura said. "I didn't find a book like that anywhere in here."

"Is there a library in town?"

"I wouldn't think the church would allow a book like that to be in a public library," C.J. said.

"Ok, not a public library," Sadie said. "Does someone in the house have a book like that?"

"Only someone interested in witches and witchcraft," Laura said.

"You mean Morag?" C.J. asked.

Sadie nodded. "Are there any other witches that you know of?"

"Greer?" Scotty asked.

"But she lives with her grandmother, so any books she has would be in their house."

"But how are we supposed to get it?" Laura asked. "They aren't just going to give it to us."

"No, they aren't."

"You want to steal it?" C.J. asked.

"We have to take things into our own hands."

"But stealing?" Scotty asked.

"Do you think they have an actual spell book?" Laura asked.

"Only one way to find out," Sadie said.

"I'm not sure about this," C.J. said.

"It's this, or wait for the knight to kill Mollie," Sadie pointed out.

C.J. looked from Scotty to Laura. Both shrugged their shoulders.

"Well," C.J. said. "As you said, it doesn't seem like they are worried about Mollie." He rubbed his chin for a moment and looked up at Sadie. "What's your plan?"

"Easy," Sadie said. "We break into Morag's house when they aren't there and find that book."

"And then?"

"And then we remove the curse ourselves."

Chapter 35

It was a beautiful sunny morning, so everyone gathered for breakfast outside on the patio, except for Maeve and Mollie.

"Are they resting in?" Sadie asked.

"Uh, yes," Walter said. "Yesterday was a terrible day for them."

Sadie shot a look at C.J., who immediately turned to his dad. "Can we go into town this morning? To walk around?"

"Sure," Angus said. "That should be fine. We're probably going into town as well."

"Really?" Sadie asked. "What for?"

"Oh, just to look around some shops," Edna told her daughter.

The kids quickly finished their breakfast and jumped up from their chairs.

"Maybe we'll see you around in town," Sadie said as they headed out the door, not waiting for a reply.

They hurried down the road toward Morag's house but slowed down when they saw it.

Not wanting to get too close to the house, they stopped and pretended to be interested in a colorful garden just off the road. Someone had stuck little signs by the various flowers with names on them, but none of the kids noticed what they said.

They concentrated on the little house down the road and whether the residents were home.

"How do we know if they are in there?" Scotty asked.

"Well, the door is closed, the windows are closed, and there is no smoke coming from the chimney," C.J. said. "That could mean they aren't there or don't want anyone to see them."

"That helps," Sadie said.

"Maybe we should get closer," Laura suggested. "Then we might hear them in the house."

They moved on to the next house on the road. The only feature of their yard was an ancient oak tree. They pretended to be interested in the old tree but felt a little awkward about it, especially when a couple of children came out of the house to play in the yard.

The children stared at them until they moved on farther down the street.

The next house was across a side street from Morag's. They worried they were getting too close not to look suspicious. They hid in an arched arbor that was the entrance to the yard at that house.

"What do we do now?" C.J. asked. "We can't just stand here all day."

"Should we walk by and watch from the other side?" Sadie asked.

It turned out that luck was on their side. Morag and Greer chose that moment to come out of their house. Greer was carrying a large basket.

"I think they're going to the market," Sadie said. "This is our chance."

When they were out of sight, the four kids left the arbor shelter and walked toward Morag's house. They watched the road to ensure the pair didn't return immediately.

"Should someone stand watch," Scotty said. "They can let us know if they come back so we can get out of the house."

"Who do you think should stand watch?" C.J. asked him.

"I could," Scotty said, "if you want me to. I'll whistle if I see them."

"Ok," C.J. said. He joined Sadie and Laura on the porch to find a way in.

They tried the door, but found it locked. There were two windows in front, but when they tested them, neither would open.

They moved to the side of the house. There was one window there, and it slid open easily.

They glanced along the street to ensure no one would see them, then boosted Laura up to the window. She crawled through and disappeared into the house.

By the time they returned to the front door, Laura had unlocked it. They ducked into the house and closed the door behind them.

"Search for any books they might have," Sadie told them as they spread out to search.

C.J. started in the tiny living room. He found knick-knacks on some shelves by the fireplace. Looking through a basket by a chair, he found knitting needles and yarn.

He found one book on a side table next to the sofa, but it wasn't a book that could help them with a curse unless it had to do with Dr. Jekyll or Mr. Hyde.

Sadie searched Greer's bedroom but had even less luck. There were no books in the room or the small wardrobe in the corner that she used as a closet. She even checked under the mattress, but there was nothing there either.

Laura was searching a room that looked like it belonged to Morag. No books were lying around or in her wardrobe, but there was a large chest at the foot of her bed.

Laura checked the chest and found it locked. She glanced around to see if there was a spot where Morag would hide a key. She remembered finding a jewelry box in the dresser's top drawer and rushed to get it out.

Inside the jewelry box were rings and necklaces, but no key. She pulled all the jewelry out and inspected the box itself. On one side, she spotted a bit of chain peeking out from under the bottom felt.

She worked the bottom up and removed it. Under the felt board was a key on a chain.

She tried the key in the chest, which unlocked with a click. She opened it up and found the inside was full of clothes.

C.J. and Sadie had finished their searches and found Laura digging through the chest of clothes when they checked on her.

Suddenly, she stopped and pulled several old books out of the heap. She laid them on the bed to search through the stack.

"Are any of them what we need?" Sadie asked.

Laura paged through several of them. "No, they're just journals about her family and a family bible." She pulled a bookmark out of one book.

"What's that?" C.J. asked.

"Berwick's Bells & Books," Laura read. "It's a bookstore in town here."

"None of the books can help us with the curse?" Sadie asked.

"None that I found," Laura said.

That's when they heard the whistle.

Chapter 36

Scotty didn't notice Greer and Morag returning until it was almost too late. He expected them to return the way they left, but they came back from a different direction.

Scotty whistled again and ducked behind some bushes near the porch. He hoped they heard him in the house, but he wasn't sure they had.

Worried they would find him in the yard, he ducked down further behind the bush.

"That was a nice little walk," Greer said as she entered the yard.

Morag shook her head. "I'm a mite older than you. I wouldn't call it a little walk."

Greer laughed. "At any rate, we're back home now." She stopped when she saw the boy's foot sticking out from behind the bush. She halted so abruptly that she almost dropped the basket of groceries.

"What's the matter, girl?" Morag asked after bumping into Greer.

"I just thought of something," Greer said, turning around and blocking her grandmother's view of the foot.

Morag's eyebrow shot up. "Thought of what?"

Greer shrugged. "Now I forgot."

"Well, let's go inside," Morag said. "I need to rest."

"Wait," Greer grabbed her grandmother's arm. "I remember now."

Greer stared into space but said nothing.

"What is it?" Morag asked.

"Eggs," Greer blurted. "Yes, eggs. We forgot to get eggs. You know how you like eggs in the morning."

"We have plenty of eggs."

"No, we don't. I dropped some this morning."

"I can live without some eggs tomorrow."

"But I want you to have your eggs. Please, Mhamó, let's go back and get you some eggs. The extra walk will do both of us some good."

Morag frowned at her granddaughter.

"Please," Greer repeated.

Morag sighed. "Fine. We can celebrate now that another MacGregor lord is dead."

Greer led her back to the street and away to the market.

Scotty peeked around the bush. When he found they had gone, he rushed to the side of the house where C.J. and Sadie had already climbed out through the window. They were helping Laura down after she pulled the window shut.

"Did you find it?" Scotty asked.

"No," Laura told him. "They don't have any books that could help us."

"It was a waste of time," Sadie said.

"Not necessarily," Laura said. She held out the bookmark. "We can check out Berwick's."

"That's right," C.J. said. "Maybe they have something that will tell us how to remove curses."

"We better go the long way," Sadie said. "We don't want to run into them on the way."

They pushed through the bushes at the side of the house and hurried down the side street.

Laura glanced at the bookmark. "It says Berwick's is on High Street. Do we know where High Street is?"

C.J. nodded. "I remember driving past it on our way back from the hospital."

He waved for them to follow him as he set out down the street.

"How far is it?" Laura asked.

"The hospital is just ahead," C.J. said over his shoulder.

The hospital came into view as they rounded a corner. They all fell silent as they remembered the events of the day before.

"It's just on the far side," C.J. said as he pushed on past the front door of the building.

They had just reached the next street when they heard familiar voices behind them.

They turned to see their parents crossing the street to the hospital door.

Scotty was just about to call his father when C.J. stopped him.

"Why are they going to the hospital again?"

"What's going on?" Sadie asked.

"Let's find out," C.J. said and headed back.

Their parents were not in the lobby when they pushed the door open. They glanced around, and Laura spotted them disappearing into the waiting room they had been in the day before.

A nurse was at the admissions desk but was busy checking a patient in. When she turned her back for a moment, the kids hurried past the desk and down the hall to the waiting room door.

Inside the waiting room, their parents stood around a doctor. They couldn't hear what he was telling them.

They ducked back when Angus glanced away from the doctor for a moment.

"Did he see us?" Scotty asked.

"I don't think so," C.J. said. "I don't think he was looking in our direction."

C.J. peeked back through the door and saw that they were all following the doctor down the hallway to the patient rooms.

"They're going with him," C.J. told the others. "We need to follow them."

They entered the now empty waiting room, and C.J. glanced down the hallway where the doctor had led them.

C.J. held his hand up to stop the others. "They're standing outside a room," he whispered.

After a few seconds, he whispered again. "They're going in."

As soon as they were all in the room, C.J. went around the corner.

"Come on!" he said.

The four made their way to the room their parents had gone into. C.J. was glad that there were no other doctors or nurses there.

They reached the door. It was open, just a crack.

"What are they saying?" Sadie asked in his ear.

"Hold on," C.J. whispered back, putting his ear to the door.

He heard several voices and tried to pick up on what they were saying.

His dad asked, "How are you doing?"

Another voice, Maeve's, he thought, said, "Better. It could have been so much worse."

Another voice, Mollie's this time, said, "Have you told the kids?"

"Not yet," Angus said. "We're worried Greer will find out."

"What about Greer?" Sadie whispered. She was leaning over C.J. with her ear as close to the door as she could.

"They haven't told us something," C.J. whispered back.

The room fell silent.

"What's going on?" Scotty asked.

The door suddenly opened, causing C.J. and Sadie to stumble back in surprise.

Angus appeared in the doorway.

He frowned at them. "What are you doing here?"

C.J. stumbled over his words, "We were... We saw..." He straightened up. "What are you doing here?"

Angus looked at the four kids and then opened the door. "I suppose it is time for you to know what's going on."

They followed him into the hospital room. The adults were all gathered around a hospital bed.

Keir grinned at them from the bed.

Chapter 37

"We're so glad you're alive," Sadie said. "How are you feeling?"

"My back still aches," Keir told them. "But I'm doing better."

"What happened?" C.J. asked.

"It was touch and go for a while there," Angus said. "The knight slashed across his back, and he lost a lot of blood."

"Luckily, the doctor stopped the bleeding," Maeve said. "Now he just needs to rest."

"But the doctor said he died," C.J. said.

"No, he didn't," Angus said. "Walter and I devised a plan to pretend he died."

"Why would you do that?" Sadie asked.

"He was still in danger," Walter said. "We needed people to believe he was dead to protect him."

"From the knight?" C.J. asked. "The knight would know if he was dead or not."

"No, it wasn't to protect him from the knight," Walter said. "There are other people we wanted to protect him from."

"Us?" Scotty asked.

"No, not any of you," Angus told him. "I noticed Greer had hung around listening at the waiting room door."

"You wanted her to think Keir was dead?" Sadie asked.

"Yes," Walter said. "Greer and her grandmother."

"You think they would want to hurt him?" C.J. asked.

"We don't know what they'd do," Angus said. "We thought it was best they thought their plan worked. That way, they wouldn't be looking for him."

"Do you think he's safe now?" Sadie asked.

"Well, if it's true that the knight can't leave the castle," Angus said, "he should be safe for the moment."

"Why did you make us think he was dead?" C.J. asked.

"We're sorry about that," Walter said. "We wanted to tell you last night, but didn't know who might be listening."

"And the way Greer is always getting into the castle," Edna said, "we decided not to tell you this morning."

"Did you think we would tell her?" C.J. asked.

"No, not on purpose," Angus said. "But if you knew he was alive, she might guess by the way you were acting."

"Or rather, you weren't acting like he died," Walter said.

"We knew something was going on," C.J. said. "Because you all weren't as worried about Mollie as we thought you should be."

Angus and Walter exchanged glances and laughed. "See how easy it is to give away a secret?" Angus asked.

"Still, you should have trusted us," Sadie said.

"I'm sorry we didn't tell you the truth," Walter said. "But it wasn't just Keir we were trying to protect."

"Who then?" C.J. asked.

"You four," Angus said. "This is a dangerous situation. We want nothing to happen to any of the four of you."

Laura went to the side of Keir's bed. "We're glad you survived. I was sad when I thought you didn't."

"Thank you," Keir said.

"Yes, that is very kind," Maeve said.

"How long will you be in the hospital?" Sadie asked.

"I don't know," Keir said.

"The doctor hasn't told us," Maeve said. "It all depends on how his injuries heal."

"For now, he is safest here," Angus said.

"What happens when he can go home?" C.J. asked Maeve. "Will you take him back to the castle?"

"We'll have to deal with that when it happens," Maeve told him. "For now, he's safest here in hospital. At least as long as the knight can't leave the castle."

"And Greer and Morag think he's dead," Walter said.

"Oh, they do," Scotty said.

"How would you know that?" Edna asked her son.

"I heard them," he said. "They celebrated he was dead." He realized what he had just said and turned to Keir. "Sorry," he said.

"You heard them? Where?" Walter asked.

"At their house," Scotty said. Sadie nudged him with her elbow. His eyes grew wide. "Uh, I was... at... their... house." He shrugged back at Sadie.

"What were you doing at their house?" Edna asked.

"We went to find out if they had something that could help remove the curse," he said quietly, "like a book or something."

"And they said that in front of you?" Walter asked.

"Well, no," Scotty said, "I was behind a bush."

"Where were the rest of you?" Angus asked. "Were you all behind a bush?"

"No," Scotty said, "they were in the house."

"Scotty!" Sadie said, "Stop talking."

Scotty blushed and looked down at his feet.

"They let you into their house?" Walter asked Sadie.

It was Sadie's turn to look down at her feet to avoid her father's gaze.

"No," C.J. said.

"You broke in?" Angus asked him.

"Well, not really," C.J. said, "a window was open."

"But you went in without their permission?"

"I guess so."

"You guess so?"

C.J. didn't want to say it, but he said in almost a whisper, "We did."

"The police could have arrested you," Edna said.

"They didn't catch us," Sadie said.

"That's not the point," Walter said. "You broke the law and could have gone to jail. You still could."

All four kids looked up at him in alarm.

"Why did you break into their house?" Angus asked.

"To see if they had a way to remove the curse," Sadie said. "We thought preventing the knight from killing someone else was worth the risk."

The adults glanced at each other silently.

"That's still not an excuse to break the law," Edna said.

The kids stood for several minutes, trying not to look at their parents.

A quiet voice finally broke the silence.

"Did you find anything?" Keir asked. His face appeared hopeful as he looked from one Young Explorer to the next.

"No," Sadie said. "We thought she'd have a book showing us how to remove it. But she didn't."

His face fell. His mother patted his arm to comfort him.

"It wasn't a total bust," Laura said. "This might help us."

She held up the bookmark from Berwick's Bells and Books.

Chapter 38

"What's that?" Edna asked.

"It's a bookmark I found," Laura said. "It's from a bookstore in town here called Berwick's Bells and Books."

"I've heard of that place," Maeve said. "It's supposed to have unusual books and odd gifts."

"Do you think it could have something about removing curses?" Laura asked her.

"I don't know. I've never been there."

"Can we go there?" Laura asked her mother.

Teresa looked at Maeve. "Do you think it's a place they could go to?"

"I would think so," she said. "It's just a gift shop, even if it's a strange one."

"What do you think, Jackson?" Teresa asked.

"Be careful," Jackson told them. "And don't be taking anything you haven't paid for."

"We won't," Laura promised. "We'll just look around."

Teresa checked with the other parents, but none had any objections.

"Be back at the castle later for supper," Teresa told them.

"We will," Sadie said. Then to Keir, she said, "We'll see you tomorrow."

"I'll probably be right here," Keir said.

When they returned to the door leading out onto the street, they carefully checked both ways to make sure there was no sign of Morag and Greer.

"Lead the way," Sadie told C.J. "You know the way to High Street."

C.J. nodded and took off down the street, with the other three trailing behind.

It only took a few minutes to find the street. It stretched off in both directions as far as they could see.

"Which way do we go?" Sadie asked.

"I don't know," C.J. said. "I just knew where the street was."

"The address is #15," Laura said, glancing at the bookmark. "The building here is 45, and the one next to it is 43. So, it's down that way," she said, pointing toward the center of town.

They found the shop three blocks away. The sign above the door had the name Berwick's Bells and Books with a bell, book, and candle around it.

The front window also had the name on it. Inside, they could see shelves of books and other knickknacks.

They went to the door, and after a glance between them, C.J. pulled open the door.

A bell above the door announced their entrance to the other people in the shop.

Several other people were browsing through the shop.

One, a tall, bald, ashen man, was looking through a table with odd, colorful bottles filled with liquid.

A woman wearing an abundance of scarves held several candles and was looking for another one as she picked through an extensive selection displayed on a tall set of shelves in the middle of the shop.

A third person was peering at several rings in a display case. Bundled up and wearing a hat, it was hard to tell if it was a man or a woman.

The man behind the counter helping with the rings, Mr. Berwick presumably, was the oldest person C.J. had ever seen. He wore what had been a very formal suit in its day. But it was currently extremely old-fashioned and faded. His white hair stuck up in every direction, and he looked down at the rings through his round spectacles perched on the end of his long nose.

They moved toward the books in the back through the rows of shelves and piles of merchandise, some of which they did not know what it was.

"Can I help you?" a rickety voice asked.

They turned to see the ancient shopkeeper with his head tilted back, looking down at them through his spectacles.

"We're just looking around," C.J. told him. "At the books."

"Something, in particular, you are looking for?"

"Uh, no, we're just looking."

"Well, if there is anything I can assist you with," he said, smiling at them with yellowed teeth. "Please let me know."

"Thank you," Sadie said. "We will."

The man returned to pulling out another set of rings for the shopper to look through. They caught him staring at them out of the corner of his eye.

When they reached the shelves of books, they searched through the titles while trying to keep a tall display of trunks between them and the shopkeeper.

There were books about poetry and books about astrology. There were books on food recipes, medicinal recipes, and even chicken and sheep feed recipes.

But there were no books about witchcraft, spells, or curses.

"Keep looking," Sadie told Laura. "We need to find something."

Laura nodded and kept looking. Sadie didn't understand many of the titles, but kept an eye out for a book that looked like it would be an old spell book.

C.J. kept watching in case the owner came to the back of the shop to help them again.

Scotty forgot all about the books as he looked through the shelves of strange objects.

He found several shelves of glass containers. He couldn't tell what was in some of them, but others contained toads, hair, and dead bugs. At least he hoped they were dead.

He was peering into another jar of dark liquid with something floating in it when C.J. touched his shoulder, startling him.

"Found anything interesting?" C.J. asked.

"Interesting? No," Scotty told him. "Scary? Yes."

They went back to find the girls. Sadie was staring at the skull of some small animal on another shelf.

"A friend of yours?" C.J. asked.

"Definitely not," Sadie said.

"Where's Laura?" Scotty asked.

"I'm over here," Laura said. "I think I found something."

She was standing next to a pedestal with a book on top of it.

The book had a cover made of what appeared to be black leather. It had thin leather straps that stretched from the front and back and tied it shut on the side.

Laura translated the title. "It says 'Curses and Maledictions.'"

Chapter 39

"Curses and Maledictions?" Scotty said. "What are maledictions?"

"Words to bring about evil or destruction," Laura told him.

"So, Curses and Curses?" Scotty asked.

Laura thought about it. "Basically," she said.

"We have to buy it," C.J. said.

"Does anyone have money?" Sadie asked.

"I've got some," C.J. said, holding out his Scottish pounds.

"So do I," Sadie told them, adding hers to the pile.

Scotty pulled his money out. "I just have dollars," he said. "I don't have any of their money."

"How about you, Laura?" Sadie asked.

Laura looked at what she had. "I have a few pounds." She added a substantial number of bills to the pile.

"How much is that?" Sadie asked.

C.J. tallied the bills in his hands. "How much do we need?"

Laura showed him the price tag on the book.

"We have plenty," he said.

"Hold on to that book," Sadie told Laura.

Laura clutched the book tightly and glanced around to see if anyone was looking.

"Don't look like you're trying to steal it," C.J. said.

Laura adjusted her grip on the book and carried it like she would carry a book to school.

"We don't want to attract attention," Sadie whispered. "We are still shopping."

They wandered around the shop, looking at some other strange objects.

They watched the other patrons to make sure no one was showing an interest in what they were doing.

The person looking at the rings finally purchased two and quickly left the store.

The woman with the candles found three more, set them on the counter, and pulled her wallet out of her purse.

"We should get a couple of other things," Laura said. "That will draw attention away from the book."

C.J. and Sadie each randomly grabbed a couple of inexpensive items.

As soon as the woman finished her candle purchase, they went to the counter and set their items in front of the shopkeeper.

"Interesting," the man said. "Let's see what we have here."

He moved the objects around on the counter and rang them up one at a time on the brass register.

"One Tarot deck," he said, pressing some buttons on the register. He pulled back a lever, and the price appeared in the register's window as a bell rang.

"Two sticks of incense," he said and repeated the process. The price in the register's window updated to the new total.

"The skin of an Adder," he said. Again, the register's bell rang.

"A snakeskin?" Scotty asked.

C.J. and Sadie shrugged.

"Snake skins are useful," the man said, "in certain circles."

He picked up the last item on the counter. "What do we have here?" He looked at the label on the jar. "Ah, Red Ant Eggs." He looked down through his spectacles at them. "Do you know how to cook them?"

Scotty covered his mouth and turned away.

"Of course," Sadie said. "Why else would we be buying them?"

The man nodded and rang the item up. "Is that everything?"

"Yes," C.J. said.

"No, wait," Laura said. "I also wanted this." She dropped the book onto the counter.

The man picked it up. He ran his hand over the cover. "Curses and Maledictions. A fascinating selection."

He put the book down again and opened it. He flipped through several pages and closed it before looking up at them again.

"Strange choice for four kids your age," the man said. "Do you know what this book is all about?"

"Of course," Sadie told him.

The bell on the door jingled, announcing that some new person had entered the shop. All four kids jumped at the sound.

They checked out the newcomer and, for a moment, thought that it was Morag, but when the old woman turned around toward them, they saw it wasn't.

When they turned back to the shopkeeper, he was peering at them again.

"You seem jumpy," the man said. "Are you having any troubles?"

"No, why do you ask?" C.J. asked.

"I was just wondering why a pleasant group of kids like you would be interested in a book like this."

They glanced around at each other.

"Bad luck," Sadie said.

"Bad luck?"

"Yes, it seems like I always have bad luck," Sadie told him. "I almost feel like I'm cursed."

"Yeah," C.J. said. "We thought maybe that book might help us get rid of her bad luck."

The man just stared at them. C.J. thought he was going to refuse to sell them the book.

"We want to turn her luck around," C.J. said. "It's hard to see everything go bad for her."

He kept staring at them for a few more moments and then nodded.

"I'm not sure this book will help, but you can try it," he said. He punched the price into the register and pulled the lever again. The register rang once more and displayed the total.

C.J. didn't have enough. They had grabbed too many other things.

"We're a pound short," he told the others. "Do any of you have one more pound?"

The other three checked their pockets but found nothing.

"I just have dollars," Scotty said. "I don't have pounds."

"Can we put something back?" C.J. asked.

"Of course," the man said. "What can you part with?"

They looked through the odd items he had rung up.

"I vote for the Red Ant Eggs," Scotty said.

"Yes," C.J. said. "Can you take the Red Ant Eggs off the total?"

The man pressed some button on the register and pulled the lever again. They had enough money for the new total.

C.J. gave him the money, and the shopkeeper opened the register. He gave him some change back and piled their purchases on the counter.

"Thank you for stopping in today," the man said.

The kids grabbed the items and hurried to the door.

"Excuse me," the man called to them.

They froze and slowly turned around.

"Good luck, young lady," the man said.

The bell rang as they opened the door and returned to the street.

They had the book.

Chapter 40

Once outside the shop, they practically ran back toward the castle. When they got close to Morag's house, they stopped running and walked until it disappeared behind them. Once they could no longer see the house, they ran again until they reached the castle.

Just as they entered the castle's front hall, a voice called out from the study's open door.

"Sadie!" Edna called. "Scotty!"

They came to a stop and crossed to the doorway.

"We're back," Sadie said as the four kids looked in at all of their parents sitting around the room.

"Did you find anything?"

"We found a book, but don't know if it will help yet."

"Do you want our help?"

"No, we're taking it to the library," Sadie told them. "We'll read through it and see if there is anything that can help us."

"Ok," Edna said. "Let us know if you do."

They said they would and hurried off to the library. Inside, they found a table where all four could look at the book and sat down to begin their examination.

Laura tried to untie the leather cord holding the covers together. The shopkeeper had tied the knot tight, and she had a tough time getting the knot to loosen up.

"Need my help?" C.J. asked.

Laura shot him a dark look.

"Just offering," he said.

Laura struggled with it for a few more minutes and then pushed the book across the table at him. "Fine, you do it then."

C.J. smiled at her. He took the knot and attempted to get it out. When he found it wasn't as easy as he thought, it was Laura's turn to smile at him.

After a couple of minutes, Sadie pulled it away from him. "For heaven's sake." It took her only a few moments to get the cord loose and remove the knot.

"I loosened it for you," C.J. told her. Everyone rolled their eyes at him.

Sadie slid the book back to Laura, who opened and paged through it.

She found the table of contents. "It looks like it's divided into three sections; How to Curse Your Enemies, Protecting Yourself from Curses, and Removing Curses."

"Turn to the Removing Curses section," Sadie told her.

She flipped through the pages until she arrived at the beginning of that section.

She read the different ways to remove a curse, looking for one that fit their needs. "Most of these are for removing curses from yourself."

"We don't need those," Sadie said.

Laura stopped turning the pages and pointed at the current one. "Here's one. It removes the curse from a place or object. Maybe that one will work."

"How do we do that?" Sadie asked.

"We'll need to get a few things for it," Laura began listing off the items one by one. "We'll need a bowl, water, salt, a candle, matches, and a garden trowel."

"They should have all of those things here," C.J. said.

"You and Scotty go find them," Sadie said, "and meet us by the gatehouse."

C.J. and Scotty went to the kitchen, where they figured they'd find almost everything on the list.

The cook was busy preparing supper and wasn't in the mood to gather any of the items for them. But a scullery maid was more than happy to take a break from her duties to get them everything on their list except for the garden trowel.

They searched for a groundskeeper and found one weeding one of the many gardens around the castle. He couldn't spare the trowel he was using but told them that there was a spare. He directed them to the tool shed.

Once they had everything they needed, the boys headed to the gatehouse, where the guards imprisoned the knight. They found the girls there waiting for them.

They wanted the guards to let them into the gatehouse, but they refused to let them in with the knight.

"We can go around to the other side," C.J. suggested. "It's close to the front grating, so we'll be as close as we need to be."

The other three agreed with him, and they quickly made their way around to the front. Even with the grating between the knight and them, they felt a little nervous being that close to it.

"Ok, what do we need to do?" Sadie asked.

Laura consulted the book. "First, we place the candle in the bowl and fill it until the water is within an inch of the top of the candle."

They placed the bowl on the ground in front of the knight with the candle in it. Laura poured the water from a pitcher until it was the correct amount.

"Now what?" C.J. asked.

"We sprinkle a handful of salt into the water."

Sadie poured salt into her hand and sprinkled it across the water's surface.

"Now we are supposed to visualize a white light flowing into the water to purify it."

They all kneeled around the bowl and tried to visualize the white light.

After a minute, Laura broke the silence. "Hopefully, that worked. Now light the candle."

Scotty struck the match and lit the candle. "Now what?"

Laura consulted the book again. "Now I say the incantation." She translated the words from Gaelic.

"Earth, Fire, Water, and Air,
be the answer to my prayer,
banish this curse and leave this pure,
tonight, I claim a blessed cure."

Laura fell silent, and no one spoke for several minutes.

"Now, we wait for the candle to burn down to the water," Laura said.

When it finally burned down far enough for the water to put it out, Laura used the trowel to dig a shallow hole. She took the candle, broke it in half, placed it in the hole, and buried it.

Taking the bowl of water, she drizzled the water out in a ring around the mound, ensuring an unbroken circle of water.

She put the bowl down and looked down at her work.

"Is that it?" C.J. asked.

"That's it," Laura said.

They looked up at the knight.

Nothing seemed different.

"Did it work?" Sadie asked.

None of them could tell.

Chapter 41

"Does the book say how to tell if we removed the curse?" Sadie asked.

Laura picked the book up and checked the instructions. "No. Nothing says how to check. It just assumes it worked."

They all looked at the knight. It still stood unmoving in the gatehouse's shadow.

"What can we do to get it to react?" C.J. asked.

"Hey, knight!" Scotty yelled at it. "Come get me!" He danced around in front of the knight, waving his arms.

The knight continued to stand there without moving.

"I think it worked," he said.

"Just because it didn't move doesn't mean it worked," C.J. told him.

"Can't we just assume it worked?" Scotty asked.

"No, we have to make sure it worked," C.J. said.

"But how do we do that?" Sadie asked.

"Can we push him and see if he falls over?" Laura suggested.

C.J. walked up close to the grate. He looked back at the other three before returning his attention to the knight.

He reached through the grating.

"C.J.!" Sadie shouted. "What are you doing?"

C.J. quickly pulled his hand back. "I was going to push him."

"What if he... does something to your arm?" Sadie asked.

C.J. thought about that. "I don't think he will. He's only after the current lord. I should be fine."

"I still don't think you should," Sadie said.

C.J. reached through the grating again. He reached as far as he could until his shoulder hit the metal and wouldn't let him go any farther. He was still a foot short of the knight.

It didn't move.

He pulled his arm back and stepped away from the grate.

"Can anyone else reach it?" he asked.

"I think you have the longest arms," Laura said.

"Maybe if I went in there," C.J. said.

"It's too dangerous," Scotty told him. "You already had to go to the hospital because of him."

"Maybe it's not dangerous anymore," C.J. said.

"We don't know that," Sadie said. "Besides, the guards wouldn't let us in before. Why would they let us in now?"

"Well, what's your big idea?" C.J. asked.

"Are there any sticks around here we can use?" Laura asked.

"Not out here," Sadie told her. "We can try to find a rake handle or something like that."

"That would work," C.J. said.

"Let's go get one," Sadie said.

When they returned to the castle, Laura's mom met them at the door.

"Time for supper," Teresa told them. "Come on in and eat."

After they sat in the dining room and the food was served, Angus asked them what they found in the book.

"We found how to remove the curse," Laura told them.

"Should we try it after supper?"

"We already did it."

Everyone stared at them.

"You should have waited for us," Edna said.

"Yes," Angus said. "Removing curses is not like baking a cake."

"It sort of was," C.J. said. "The directions were pretty clear."

"What happened?" Walter asked. "Did it work?"

"That's the problem," Sadie said. "When it was done, nothing happened. It's still just standing there."

"Well, let's finish our supper," Teresa said, "and we'll all go down and see what we can find out."

They finished the meal in silence. Everyone wondered whether it removed the curse and what it meant to the MacGregor family.

After finishing the meal, they sent for Quinn and headed down to the gatehouse to see the knight.

Everyone except C.J. He took a detour to the tool shed and collected a long-handled rake.

When he got to the gatehouse, he found everyone had gone outside to examine the knight at close range.

Quinn arrived a few minutes later, and they filled him in on what was happening.

They stood staring at the knight, trying to think of a way to test if the kids had removed the curse.

"We thought if we pushed him over and it didn't stand up again, that might mean we removed the curse," C.J. said.

"He tried to reach in a push it," Scotty said. "But he couldn't reach."

"You put your arm in there?" Angus asked.

C.J. blushed. "Nothing happened."

"You don't know what could have happened," Angus told him. "Don't take risks like that."

"Well, since I couldn't reach it," C.J. said, "I thought we could use a rake to knock it over." He held out the rake.

Quinn took it from the boy and took it over to the portcullis.

He slid the handle through the grating and toward the knight. It was long enough to tap the breastplate, but not long enough to push it.

After several attempts to hit it hard enough to topple it, Quinn gave up and pulled the handle back out.

"That was a good thought," he said. "Just a mite short."

"Any other ideas short of going inside there?" Angus asked.

Everyone shook their heads.

"Let me get something," Quinn said. He headed back to the castle.

"When he tapped it with the rake, it didn't react," Sadie said. "Could that mean we removed the curse?"

"I don't know what would conclusively show you removed the curse," Angus said.

"Yes," Edna said. "We must be sure before Keir can return to the castle."

Quinn returned from the castle carrying a rifle.

"What's that for?" Walter asked.

Quinn carefully loaded the rifle before he spoke. "Everyone stand away from the portcullis."

He walked up to the grating and rested the barrel on one crossbar at his eye level.

Placing the stock at his shoulder, he looked down the sight at the knight. With a loud bang, he fired. The recoil caused him to take a step back from the grating.

The bullet hit the knight and caused it to fall back onto the floor of the gatehouse.

It didn't move.

Chapter 42

Nobody moved for several minutes. They stood staring at the knight sprawled on the ground, its sword lying at its feet.

"Is it... dead?" C.J. asked.

"I couldn't kill it," Quinn said. "I just wanted to see if it would react to an attack. And it didn't."

"The curse may be gone," Angus said. "Or it just may be dormant until Keir returns."

"Do you think it's safe for Keir to return to the castle?" Scotty asked.

"I don't know," Angus told him.

"There's only one way to find out," Quinn said. "We need to bring him back and see how the knight reacts. Or doesn't."

"We'll have to talk to Maeve," Angus said. "It's a risk to bring Keir back here. She'll have to decide whether she wants him to come back."

"We can talk to her in the morning," Quinn said. "It's too late for Keir to come back tonight."

Angus agreed.

They made their way back into the castle.

In the morning, the kids were up early and full of energy. They met their parents on the way down from their rooms.

"Are we bringing Keir back before breakfast?" Scotty asked.

"No," Walter said. "We'll have breakfast first. After that, we'll head into town and talk to Maeve."

They devoured their breakfast, but then had to wait while the adults finished theirs. They weren't as eager to rush to town as the kids were.

When everyone finished, Walter, Angus, and the kids headed to the courtyard to meet Quinn, who brought the car around. They all piled in and headed for town.

"Do you think she'll let him return to the castle?" C.J. asked.

"She is protective of her kids," Quinn said. "But if that's the only way to find out about the curse, I think she'll allow it."

They pulled up in front of the hospital. The kids jumped out as soon as the car came to a stop.

"Wait a minute," Angus called to the kids. They let the hospital door close and turned back.

"Let Walter and me talk to Maeve first and give her time to think about her decision," Angus said. "We don't want you to overwhelm her with your energy."

"You can stay in the waiting room until we've talked to her," Walter said. "We'll call you in afterward."

"Ok," C.J. said, kicking at the ground with his foot. The other three kids also reluctantly agreed.

The kids followed Angus and Walter into the hospital and to the waiting room. After getting the kids settled, they went down the hall to Keir's room.

When Walter returned to the waiting room, he said, "Come on back."

They followed him to Keir's room, where they found Keir asleep. Maeve sat beside him while Mollie appeared asleep in a chair with a blanket over her.

C.J. got right to the point. "Are you letting him return to the castle?" he asked.

"I'm willing to let him go back," she told him. "I know it's dangerous, but we need to know if he's still under the curse."

"But we haven't talked to Keir yet," Quinn said. "He gets a say in this, too."

"We'll let him rest, and when he wakes up, we'll find out how he feels about it," Maeve said.

They waited in the waiting room for about an hour until he woke up.

Maeve explained what they had in mind. "Would you be up to going back to the castle to see if the knight is no longer cursed?" she asked when she was done.

"I don't know," Keir told her. "Will it come after me again?"

"We locked it back up in the gatehouse," Quinn said. "If it tries to come after you, we'll bring you back into town."

"It's the only way to see if it's safe for you to return to the castle," Angus told him.

Keir thought about it for a while. "I want to go back home," he said. "If that's the only way to know if the curse was removed, I guess I have to."

Quinn suggested that they all return to the castle while Keir gets discharged. He'll go back for him, Mollie, and Maeve when they're ready.

They were waiting outside the gatehouse when Quinn pulled up outside the castle. Keir waited for Quinn to open the car door before getting out. He winced as he stood up.

"Are you ok?" C.J. asked.

"My back still hurts," Keir told him. He looked into the shadows of the gatehouse. "Is it still in there?"

"Yes," Sadie said. "But it's not moving. Quinn shot it, and now it's lying on the ground."

Keir slowly moved to the grating and looked in. Maeve and Mollie joined him at the entrance. The knight didn't move.

"Does that mean the curse is gone?" Keir asked.

"It's hopeful," Walter told him. Walter turned to Quinn. "Try driving him onto the grounds to the other side of the gatehouse."

Keir and his family got back into the car. Quinn drove through the western gate and into the courtyard. The others followed them on foot.

When they arrived at the gatehouse again, Quinn stood by the car, but Keir was still inside.

"How does it look?" Angus asked him.

"Still no movement," Quinn said.

"Ready?"

"I am. I'm not sure Keir is."

"Let's see what happens," Angus said.

Quinn opened the doors for Maeve and Mollie first. Then he opened Keir's door.

When everyone was ready, he escorted them toward the gatehouse. Keir walked slowly, hiding behind Quinn.

They couldn't see the knight inside. The shadows were too dark.

They heard a chilling sound when they were within a few feet of the portcullis.

It was the sound of metal moving. Before they could react, they heard the pounding of metal feet, and the knight quickly loomed out of the shadows.

He ran straight at the grating and slammed into it full force. Its sword slid through one hole in the grating. It came just inches from Quinn when its shoulder hit the portcullis.

They had not removed the curse.

Chapter 43

Several people screamed. Quinn backed up, almost knocking Keir down. He quickly turned and grabbed the boy before he fell.

Everyone backed away from the grating, out of the reach of the knight's sword.

The knight pulled the sword back through the portcullis and stood waiting.

"I thought you got rid of the curse?" Keir shouted.

"We thought we did," Sadie told him.

"Obviously, we didn't," C.J. said.

"Is he going to get out of there?" Keir asked Quinn.

"No, he's not getting out."

"I don't want to be here," Keir said.

"Keir has to leave," Maeve called to Quinn. "He's still not safe here."

"Do I go back to the hospital?" Keir asked.

"No," Maeve told him. She called to Quinn, "We need to take him to the house."

"I thought you were going to take him out of the castle?" C.J. asked.

"We are," Quinn said. "The house is a place in town that we set up for the MacGregors in case Keir couldn't come back here."

"We have to get back in the car," Quinn called out.

C.J. and Sadie grabbed Keir and helped him back to the car. Maeve grabbed Mollie, and Quinn hurried them back toward the car as well.

Quinn helped Maeve and Mollie into the car. C.J. opened the door for Keir, and all three piled in.

Quinn jumped into the driver's seat and spun the vehicle around. He headed for the western gate again, leaving the rest of them to deal with the knight.

The knight moved to the outside portcullis of the gatehouse as the car drove by and turned onto the drawbridge.

It stood motionless as the car returned to the town.

As Quinn sped down the road into town, Maeve cautioned him, "Slow down. We don't want to attract attention."

"Sorry, Ma'am," Quinn said and slowed to a more reasonable speed.

Sadie noticed Keir leaning against his mother. "Are you ok?"

"That was scary," he whispered.

Maeve put her arm around him. "It was scary for all of us," she said.

"Watch out!" C.J. cried out. "Greer is up ahead."

They saw Greer walking along the street ahead of them. When she heard the car approaching, she turned.

"Duck down," Sadie told Keir. "We don't want her to discover you're still alive."

Keir slid down in his seat until his head was below window level.

After passing the girl, C.J. looked back at her. She briefly watched the car and then hurried down the street after it.

"She's following us," C.J. announced.

"It's not too far from the house," Quinn said. "We have to lose her."

"Stop at Donella's," Maeve told him. "Mollie and I will pretend to shop. You stay in the car with Keir."

Quinn pulled over in front of a clothing store on the next block. The sign above the door proclaimed it to be Donella's Clothiers.

"Sadie and I can keep Greer busy," C.J. said. "After you shop for a few minutes, you can go to the house. We'll stay here."

"We can find you later," Sadie said.

"Ok," Maeve agreed. "Turn at the next corner. We'll be down a few blocks on the right, number 33."

The four of them got out of the car. Mollie and Maeve went into the shop while C.J. and Sadie pretended to notice Greer coming down the street toward them.

"Hello, Greer," C.J. called.

"What are you doing here?" Greer asked.

"Maeve and Mollie needed to shop for an outfit," Sadie said.

"For the funeral," C.J. added.

"What are you doing?" Sadie asked Greer.

"I, uh, I'm shopping too," Greer said. "My grandmother needs some more yarn."

C.J. nodded. "She knits?"

"Yes, she enjoys knitting us things," Greer told them. "Are you shopping too?"

"We just wanted to get out of the castle," Sadie said. "We came along when they said they wanted to come into town."

The shop door opened. Mollie and Maeve came out. They glanced at Greer but said nothing.

"Hello, Mrs. MacGregor," Greer said.

"Greer," Maeve acknowledged her.

"They had nothing you wanted?"

"Not today."

When they approached the car and were ready to open the door, C.J. and Sadie stepped in front of Greer to prevent her from seeing Keir inside.

"Do you want to go to the yarn shop?" Sadie asked C.J., "We could do some shopping with Greer."

"We could go there," C.J. said.

Once they were in the car, Quinn pulled away and headed down the street.

"Aren't you going with them?" Greer asked.

"No, we're going with you," Sadie told her.

"You wouldn't be interested in yarn," Greer said.

"Maybe not," C.J. said. He turned to Sadie. "Maybe we could go to that candy shop we saw the other day."

"That sounds fun," Greer said.

"Do you want to go with us?" Sadie asked.

"No, I have my shopping to do."

"I guess we'll see you later," C.J. said.

"I guess so," Greer said.

C.J. and Sadie started down the street in the candy store's direction. They glanced over their shoulders and saw Greer going past the yarn shop toward her house.

When they reached the corner, they ducked around it and hurried down the street to #33.

They found the car parked in front of the house. Everyone was still inside.

Quinn got out when he saw them walk up. "Did you get rid of her?"

"Yes," C.J. said. "She went back home."

"Good. Let's get everyone inside."

Quinn opened the door for Mollie, Maeve, and Keir. They hurried up to the entrance of the house. Quinn unlocked the door and let them all in.

When the door closed, the street was quiet again.

All except for a young girl peeking around the corner at the house.

"He's alive!" Greer said under her breath.

Chapter 44

After sunset, when darkness had settled in around the castle, a lone figure walked along the outside of the castle wall. It paused near the western gate, but the closed door meant the figure needed to find another entrance.

It continued along the wall and stopped at a point where it bent. Feeling along the stones at the bend, it found a couple of handholds and climbed the wall.

At the top, it swung its legs over the wall, found the footholds it was looking for, and climbed down to the other side.

At the bottom, it dropped its backpack on the ground. It landed with a jangle of metal.

Greer pulled her mask off and glanced around the courtyard. There were lights in the castle, but the only lights in the courtyard were where the guards stood guarding the knight.

She pulled off her dark over-clothes, revealing a scullery maid's uniform underneath. She unzipped the backpack and removed two containers. One was a tub of biscuits, and the other was a water flask.

Earlier in the day, she baked some biscuits for her grandmother. But her grandmother didn't know she baked a second batch of the biscuits adding a sleeping draught. She added a second sleeping draught to the flask of water.

Tucking the backpack against the base of the wall, she hurried across the courtyard to the castle wall. She made her way around toward the front of the castle and then walked boldly out toward the guards at the gate.

"What are you doing out here?" one guard asked when she got close.

"Cook sent me out with a little something for you," Greer said.

"What do you have there?" the other guard asked.

"Some shortbread biscuits," she said, holding up the tub. She held out the flask. "And a bit to drink."

The first guard took the flask. "I need some of this," he said, taking a draught. He started choking on it. Finally, he got out a few words. "That's not ale."

"No, it's water," she told them. "You think Cook would send you out ale when you're on duty?"

"The biscuits better be good," the second guard said as he reached into the tub and grabbed two of them.

Greer held the tub out to the first guard, who took two biscuits.

"Has it moved?" she asked them.

"Nah," the first guard said, spitting bits of the biscuit at her as he spoke. "Not since the young Lord was here earlier today."

"They brought him back here?"

"Didn't you know?" the guard asked.

"I was visiting my family. I didn't get back to the castle until this evening," she told them.

Both guards grabbed another couple of biscuits from the tub.

"I didn't know I was this hungry," the first one said.

"Are they good?" Greer asked.

"They're good but dry," the second guard said. He grabbed the flask and drank deeply.

"That's an understatement," the first guard said. He took the flask from his compatriot and gulped it down.

"We're going to need more water," the second guard told her.

"I'll fetch some right away," she told them, heading toward the castle. Once she crossed the courtyard, she went to where she had stashed her backpack.

When she returned to the gatehouse, the two guards were asleep. She opened the backpack and pulled several lengths of chains from inside and replaced them with the tub and flask.

Heading up the stairs to the room above the gatehouse, she located the winch that operated the inside portcullis and raised it a little. Once she raised it as far as she needed, she returned to the courtyard.

She shined her flashlight into the gatehouse. The knight was still standing by the front portcullis, facing the drawbridge. Laying down, she slid under the portcullis. She hadn't raised it quite enough and flattened herself extra thin to slip past the spikes at the bottom.

She grabbed the chains she had deposited by the grating and pulled them under.

Once inside, she set her flashlight on the ground, facing the knight. Watching for any sudden movement, she carefully moved toward it.

Separating the four chains, she carefully laid them near the knight. She checked to ensure she had the four locks to connect the chains when she wrapped them around it.

She took the first chain and lock. Kneeling behind the knight, she reached one end of the chain around the legs of the knight and grabbed it with her other hand. She pulled the chain tight around its knees and hooked the shackle through one link. She got the other end of the chain attached to the shackle when everything went sideways.

The knight turned, pulling the lock out of Greer's hands. Its sword swung at her and hit her with the flat of the blade, causing her to tumble to the side.

It stepped toward her, but the chain prevented its legs from moving. It fell forward and landed on its face. The sword tumbled out of its hand and slid toward Greer.

Greer grabbed the sword and got to her feet. The knight flipped onto its back and grabbed the chain still wrapped around its knees.

She sprinted toward the portcullis and almost reached it when a chain slammed into the back of her head.

Falling forward onto the grating, she slid down and rolled onto her back to slide under the portcullis. Her vision got blurry. She looked back and saw the knight striding toward her.

She tried to make herself slide under the grating but couldn't seem to move her body. As the knight approached her, a darkness fell over her, and she lost consciousness.

Chapter 45

Quinn returned from the house well after dark. He pulled the car around to the western gate and honked the horn. He was tired. It seemed forever before the wooden gate swung in.

When he passed into the castle, he raised his hand to acknowledge the guard. The guard saluted him and began closing the gate again after he passed.

He turned and drove to the front of the castle and the main gate. As he approached, the car's headlights lit the area by the entrance.

When he saw the guards lying on the ground and the portcullis partially up, he hit the brakes and parked the car by the gate.

He jumped out and ran to the guards. Checking each one, he let out a breath when he discovered they were not dead.

He tried to rouse them, but they did not wake up.

Grabbing the flashlight from one guard, he shined the light into the gatehouse.

The knight stood motionless in the middle of his prison, looking out of the castle.

He hurried back to the car and honked the horn several times before returning to the prostrate guards.

He found a half-eaten biscuit next to one guard. Picking it up, he examined it briefly before putting it in his jacket pocket.

The two guards from the western gate ran up to him.

"What happened to them?" one of them asked.

"I don't know," Quinn said. "I found them like this."

"Did they fall asleep?" the other guard asked.

"This is more than just falling asleep," Quinn said. "I think someone knocked them out."

"Malcolm," he said to the first guard, "Go up and close that portcullis."

Malcolm hurried up the steps.

"Tavish," he said to the other, "go inside and call the doctor. These two are alive, and I want them to stay that way."

As Tavish ran toward the castle, the grating fell back into place.

When Malcolm returned, he investigated the dark gatehouse. "Is it still in there?"

"Yes," Quinn said. He walked over to the portcullis, reached through it, and retrieved a length of chain lying on the ground inside it.

"What is this doing here?" he asked himself out loud.

Tavish came running back from the castle. "The doctor is on his way," he said, panting.

"Go back to the west gate and let him in when he gets here," Quinn told them.

After they left, he shined his flashlight at the knight again, but it hadn't moved.

He moved the light around in the gatehouse. Three more chains were lying on the ground around where the knight stood. And there was something else.

A dark mound was in front of the knight. The knight was standing between Quinn and the mound, so he couldn't get a good look at it.

A car passed over the drawbridge. Its headlights briefly shone in Quinn's eyes as it turned toward the other gate.

A few minutes later, the car pulled up next to Quinn's. The doctor grabbed a bag from the back seat and hurried over to the man. When he saw the two men lying on the ground, he kneeled beside one without a word.

After he checked both men, he stood back up and looked down at them. "Someone's drugged them," he said. "I can't tell what it was, but it was some sort of sedative."

They heard someone groan. The doctor rechecked each man but shook his head. "They are still out," he said. "It wasn't them."

When they heard a second groan, Quinn realized it was coming from inside the gatehouse. He shined his torch inside once again.

It startled him to see the mound by the knight move and a leg stretched out from it.

"Hello?" Quinn called out. "Can you hear me?"

The mound moved a bit, and a second leg stretched out. The person was lying on their back.

"Are you conscious?" The doctor called.

A tiny voice said something that they couldn't hear. Then they made out the words, "I'm scared."

"We're here," Quinn told her. "Can you move?"

"A little," the voice said. "It hurts."

"Hold on," Quinn said. "We're coming around to that side."

He and the doctor ran to the western gate. Quinn told the guards there to open the gate and leave it open.

Once the gate was open, he told them to head to the main gate and prepare to open the front portcullis.

When they reached the main gate, Quinn shined the flashlight at the body on the ground.

"Are you still with us?" Quinn asked.

The person rolled her head toward the light, and Quinn immediately recognized Greer.

"I'm still here," Greer said weakly.

"Are you able to move?"

"Yes, but I'm scared to."

"I understand," Quinn said. "If we raise the portcullis, can you make it here?"

"I... I think so," she told him.

He looked past the knight and saw a figure at the other end of the gatehouse.

"Malcolm?" he called.

"It's Tavish," the figure said. "Malcolm is up above."

"When I say," Quinn called, "Yell up to Malcolm to raise the portcullis half a meter, no more."

"Yes, sir," Tavish said.

"Ok, Greer," Quinn said, keeping his voice as calm as possible. "When the grate goes up, run toward me as fast as you can, ok?"

Greer's voice was weak but clear. "Ok."

Quinn took several breaths. "Tavish," Quinn said. "Raise the portcullis."

They heard Tavish call up to Malcolm, and soon the grating rose.

"Now, Greer, go!"

Greer rolled over and got to her feet. She stumbled toward the grating as it slowly rose.

She covered half the distance to the portcullis before the knight moved.

Quinn saw the movement. "Greer, run faster. You're almost there."

She picked up a little speed. The knight strode toward her.

"I don't know if she'll make it," the doctor whispered to Quinn.

Quinn kneeled on the ground next to the grating. He held his arms out to the girl.

The knight was almost on her when she dove toward the opening. When she was within Quinn's reach, he grabbed her. He pulled her out and rolled away from the portcullis. The knight tried to reach through but couldn't touch them.

"Drop the gate!" Quinn yelled. A moment after hearing Tavish echo his command to Malcolm, the gate fell into place, preventing the knight from sliding under.

Chapter 46

The knight stood motionless again. It faced them with its helmet almost touching the grating, its sword held in its hand, and the blade in the dirt.

Quinn let Greer roll freely onto her back. She, too, was motionless. Her eyes were closed, and her head lolled to one side.

"Doctor," Quinn called out. "She's out again."

The doctor rushed over to her and checked her vital signs. "She's breathing, and her heart rate is normal."

"Should we get her to hospital?" Quinn asked.

"Definitely," the doctor said. "I'll go get my car."

The doctor hurried off to the other gate to get back into the castle.

When he returned, Quinn picked up Greer, placed her in the back seat, and let her lie across it.

"Tavish!" Quinn called.

"Yes, Sir?" Tavish called back.

"The Doctor and I are taking Greer to hospital. Let the American MacGregors know what's happened."

"Yes, Sir," Tavish said, heading across the courtyard to the castle.

Quinn jumped into the car's passenger side, and the Doctor headed off across the drawbridge and toward the town.

The car barely stopped in front of the hospital before Quinn popped open the door and jumped out. He pulled open the rear door and carefully lifted Greer out.

"She's still out," Quinn said as the doctor held the hospital doors for him.

The doctor led him to Accident and Emergency, where they placed Greer on an examination table.

"You should wait outside," the doctor told Quinn. Quinn monitored the people working on Greer as he backed out of the room.

Quinn was sitting in the waiting room when Walter and Edna arrived. Angus and the kids followed them in.

"Is Greer all right?" Edna asked.

Walter didn't wait for the answer. "What happened?"

Quinn held his hands up. "Please, why don't we all sit down, and I'll tell you what I know."

He waited for everyone to sit down in the waiting room. Once they settled, he began.

"We found Greer unconscious in the gatehouse with the knight. I don't know why she was there, but apparently, she snuck into the castle and made her way there."

"What about the guards?" Angus asked.

"She drugged them," Quinn said. "They were asleep when I arrived."

"How is she?" Walter asked.

"I don't know," Quinn said. "They've been examining her but haven't told me anything yet."

"Has anyone told Morag?" Edna asked.

"No," Quinn told her. "I'll call and have someone from the castle head over there."

"One of us should tell her," Angus said.

"I'll go," Edna said. "Have you told Maeve?"

"Yes, I called her as soon as they had me leave the room," Quinn said. "She and the kids are coming here soon."

"Good," Edna said. "I'll be back with Morag as soon as I can."

Not long after Edna left, the doctor entered the waiting room to talk to them. Everyone stood and gathered around him.

"She's stable," the doctor said. "She's had a concussion. There's a contusion on her head where something heavy hit her."

"A heavy chain?" Quinn asked.

The doctor thought for a moment. "Yes, that would be a possibility. She'll have to stay in hospital for a few days until we're sure she has no additional symptoms."

The doctor looked around at all the faces. "Are any of you family?"

"No," Quinn said. "We've sent for her grandmother. But she isn't here yet."

The waiting room door opened, and Maeve entered, along with Keir and Mollie.

"How is she?" Maeve asked.

Quinn filled her in on Greer's status. He also told her that Edna had gone to inform Morag.

"Has she said anything about why she was there?" Maeve asked.

"She is still unconscious," the doctor said. "I'll let you know when she wakes up."

They thanked the doctor, and he went back to Greer's room.

"Was she there trying to release the knight again?" Maeve asked.

"The portcullis was up enough for her to get in. But it was not enough for the knight to get out," Quinn said.

"Why else would she be there?"

"There were several chains," Quinn told her. "But it's hard to say what she was doing with them."

"Could she have been trying to tie up the knight with the chains?" Angus asked.

"Maybe," Quinn said. "But what was she going to do with it, then?"

"We can wonder about her motives all night," Walter said. "We won't know anything until she regains consciousness."

"And maybe not even then," Maeve said. "We can't trust the girl."

"Did the knight attack her?" C.J. asked.

"It looks like it," Quinn said.

"It never attacked her before. Did it think she was working against it, so it turned on her?"

"Does the knight think at all?" Maeve asked.

"It knew to hide among the other suits of armor in the armor room," Sadie said. "It seems to make plans on its own."

"We'll just have to wait and see what she says," Walter said.

C.J. was going to say something more when they heard the doctor calling for help in Greer's room.

Several doctors and nurses rushed into the room.

Everyone sat back down, and no one said anything more. They could hear sounds coming from her room, but couldn't make out any words.

After a long time, it became quiet, and soon they began filing out of the room.

"Is that good or bad?" Sadie asked.

"It didn't sound good," Walter told her. "But we can hope."

The doctor appeared in the waiting room.

"What happened?" Maeve asked.

The doctor looked around at their faces. "Her blood pressure dropped. It was touch and go, but we stabilized her."

"Is she going to be all right?" Maeve asked.

"I believe so," the doctor said. "But we want to keep her in hospital for a few days."

"Is she still unconscious?" Quinn asked.

"She regained consciousness once we stabilized her."

Chapter 47

"Can we see her?" Maeve asked.

"She's frail," the doctor told her. "She should have some rest."

"Of course. We can talk to her later."

"Talk to her about what?" a voice croaked from the doorway.

Morag and Edna had entered the waiting room. Morag crossed the room and stood right in front of Maeve.

"What do you have to talk to Greer about?" she said.

"We'd like to know what she was doing at the castle," Maeve said.

"I don't want you anywhere near her," Morag said. "Leave her be. And me too."

She turned her back on Maeve and confronted the doctor.

"I want to see my granddaughter," she demanded.

"Your granddaughter needs some rest," the doctor told her. "She's been through a traumatic experience and doesn't need a lot of excitement around her."

"You can't keep me from seeing her!"

"I didn't say you can't see her. But if you want to see her, you must calm down and stop shouting. Making a fuss will not help your granddaughter."

Morag stood and stared at the doctor.

"Do you want to see her?"

Morag nodded. "Yes," she said in a much calmer tone.

"Very well," the doctor said. "Follow me."

The doctor led her back to Greer's room.

Edna sat down with the others. She let out a sigh.

"How was she when you told her?" Walter asked.

"Upset, of course. She also accused us of hurting Greer out of revenge."

"Did you tell her about where she was? And the knight?"

"I did. But she's hell-bent on blaming MacGregors for anything that happens. She won't listen to reason."

"I don't think she ever will," Maeve said. "Her hatred consumes her."

"She needs to let that go. It's already almost killed her granddaughter," Walter said.

Morag was causing a scene in Greer's room. Moments later, several attendants rushed into the room. Raised voices down the hall interrupted them.

When they returned to the hall, they were physically escorting Morag out of the room.

They released her as soon as they were in the waiting room, but they blocked her from returning to her granddaughter's room.

The doctor returned a few minutes later and dismissed the attendants.

"I told you not to disturb your granddaughter," the doctor told her.

"I'll be taking my granddaughter out of here," Morag told him. "Before you do anything more to make her worse."

The doctor leaned in toward her. "Your granddaughter is in rough shape. She has almost died once. We want to ensure she is out of danger before you take her home."

"You can't tell me what I can and can't do. I'll take her out of this place if I want to. And there's nothing you can do about it."

"They are trying to help Greer," Maeve told her.

Morag turned on her. "And you're trying to kill her!"

"We're not trying to hurt you or your granddaughter," Edna said. "We're trying to help you both."

"By bashing her on the head?"

"We didn't hurt her. The fact is, we rescued her after it attacked her," Quinn said. "If we hadn't, we don't know what it would have done to her."

"It?" Morag asked.

"The knight," Quinn said. "We found her in the gatehouse with the knight standing over her. She was barely conscious, and when she moved so we could help her, the knight tried to attack her again."

"Why would the knight attack her?"

"I don't know," Quinn said. "That's what we need Greer to tell us."

"That's ridiculous," Morag said. "Hestor cursed the knight to kill MacGregor lords. It wouldn't do anything to harm Greer."

"Maybe it also attacks anyone who tries to prevent it from carrying out the curse," Walter said. "Maybe your granddaughter tried to stop it, and it turned on her."

"She wouldn't try to stop it," Morag said. "Anyone who says so is a liar."

"You don't control the knight," Angus told her. "The knight works on its own. And it looks like it will do anything it needs to fulfill the curse, including harming Greer."

"It wouldn't hurt Greer," Morag said. "No matter what you say."

"But it did," Greer called from her room.

They all turned to find Greer, barely standing up in the hallway.

Several people rushed to help her. Maeve and Edna were the first to reach her. They held her up so she wouldn't fall to the floor.

They helped her back into her room, and she sat on the edge of the bed. Everyone gathered around her in her room.

"You should get some rest," the doctor said.

Greer ignored the doctor and faced her grandmother. "They are telling you the truth. The knight attacked me."

"You're confused. The knight wouldn't attack you. They did," Morag said, pointing at Maeve.

"Mhamó!" Greer said. She was still too weak to shout, but the one word stopped her grandmother. "You must listen to me. Sit down."

Angus brought a chair into the room. Morag sat down near her granddaughter.

"This curse has gone too far," Greer said. "It has killed one person who didn't deserve it. And it almost killed two other people, including me."

"Two?" Morag asked, barely audible.

Greer pointed to Keir, who had been hiding behind his mother.

"You?" Morag said.

"Yes," Greer said. "I hated this curse when I thought it had killed him. He doesn't deserve to die, either."

"But he's a MacGregor," Morag said.

"It doesn't matter. Gavin was the only MacGregor who did anything against our family, and he's long gone."

Morag looked down at the floor.

Greer continued. "The curse isn't killing just the MacGregors." She reached for Morag's hand and clasped it. "It's killing our family, too."

Morag squeezed her hand.

"I went to the castle to chain it up. It seemed to know what I was trying to do. It turned on me."

She leaned forward toward her grandmother. "Believe me. The knight tried to kill me."

Chapter 48

Morag released Greer's hand and stood up. She turned away from the girl.

"I can't believe it," Morag said. "It can't be true. Why would it hurt us? We're the ones it is avenging."

"It isn't avenging us," Greer said. "It's avenging Hestor. She never considered us."

Morag whirled on her. "Don't you talk about her like that."

"Why not? She never knew about us," Greer said, "And we know very little about her. She is little more than an idea handed down from generation to generation. And that idea is killing us, too."

"You don't know what you're talking about," Morag said. "They hit you on the head, and now you're just confused."

She turned to the doctor. "That bump on her head could confuse her, couldn't it?"

"Well, yes," the doctor said. "It could cause confusion."

"See, I told you."

"But, in this case, she shows no signs of confusion. She sounds very lucid."

"Lucid?" Morag asked.

"Rational," the doctor said. "She makes perfect sense."

"Did you get hit on the head, too?" Morag asked.

"Just because someone disagrees with you doesn't mean they're confused or don't know what they are saying," the doctor said.

"My head hurts, but I'm thinking clearer than I have in a long time," Greer told her. "I've watched you waste your life with this hatred of the MacGregors, and it needs to stop."

"I haven't wasted my life," Morag protested.

"What about Mom and Dad?" Greer asked. "They barely spoke to you for years because of this obsession. I rarely could see you. They only let me stay with you because they had no one to take care of me when they went to war."

Morag opened her mouth to respond, but no words came out.

"This curse is out of control," Greer continued. "I don't know how many people it hurt in our family's history, but I know it hurt you, then Mom, and now me. It must stop."

"I didn't want it to hurt you," Morag said.

"I know you didn't." Greer closed her eyes. She exhaled and took a deep breath.

"How are you doing?" the doctor asked.

"My head aches," she said. "And I'm tired."

"I think you should get some rest. This is not good for your recuperation."

"No," Greer said. "This is important." She leaned forward again and looked up at her grandmother.

"Mhamó, I love you," Greer said. "I don't blame you for this."

Morag's eyes became wet. "I never wanted it to hurt you. I lost your mom in the war." She fell silent and looked out the little window at the gray skies.

She looked at her granddaughter. "No, I lost her long before that. You are the only family I have left."

"You haven't lost me," Greer told her.

"I almost lost you. All because you couldn't come to me about your plans to get rid of the knight."

"I'm still here. Maybe we can work together to get rid of this curse. We can put an end to the hatred and death." She retook her grandmother's hand. "Together."

Morag held her hand for several minutes, saying nothing. Finally, she stood and let her hand go.

She paced around the room.

Greer laid back on the bed and closed her eyes. The doctor touched her shoulder, and she reopened her eyes. She looked up at him and smiled. "I'm fine."

The doctor nodded and let her close her eyes again.

As Morag paced around the room, she paused when she passed Keir and looked down at him. Keir leaned closer to his mother.

When she returned to Greer, she stopped and sat by her again.

"My mother taught me about the curse. I learned to hate the MacGregors from her."

"I know," Greer said softly.

"It's all I've known since I was a young girl," Morag continued. "When she was dying, she made me promise to find the knight and set him free."

"That was unfair to you," Greer said.

"But I tried to do the same to your mother and you."

"Let it go now."

"It's hard," Morag admitted.

"I know," Greer said.

Maeve walked over to where Morag was sitting. Morag stood quickly and backed away.

Maeve opened her hands. "I bear you no ill will, Morag."

Morag stopped backing away but still stood stiffly.

"You are a victim just as we are," Maeve told her. "I want to offer you peace. I don't want this feud to go on any longer."

Morag looked at Greer, who nodded to her.

Maeve held out her hand. "Will you take my hand and make it a time of peace between our families?"

She stood looking at Maeve's hand, reaching out to her. Greer looked at her, not knowing what her grandmother would do.

Everyone in the room was on the edge of their seat, waiting.

Morag wiped her hand on her dress and slowly extended her hand. When she clasped Maeve's hand, and they shook, everyone started breathing again.

"Thank you, Morag," Maeve said. "I know how difficult that was. I hope I can show you I am truly sincere."

"Now we just have to put this curse behind for all of us," Greer said. "Before any more people get hurt."

"Yes," Morag said. "I'm ready to give up this burden. I am so tired."

"We want to help you all we can," Maeve said.

"What do we need to do to remove the curse?" Sadie asked her.

Morag looked at Sadie in surprise. "What do you mean?"

"You know how to remove the curse. We'll help you," Sadie said.

"You think I know how to remove the curse?" Morag asked, glancing around at all the faces staring at her.

"Of course," Sadie said. "Your family put the curse on the knight. Don't you know how to remove it?"

"I'm no witch," Morag said. "I don't know how to remove the curse."

Chapter 49

"You don't know how to remove the curse?" Sadie asked in shock.

"No," Morag said. "I know nothing about how curses work. Do you?"

Sadie blushed. "No. We found a book on removing curses and tried to do it ourselves."

"And?" Morag asked. "How did that go?"

"It didn't work," Sadie whispered.

"I probably would do just as well," Morag said. "Just because my kin created the curse doesn't mean she told anyone how to remove it."

"If you can't remove it, who can?"

"If you wanted to make friends with me so I would remove the curse," Morag said with a laugh, "you wasted your time."

"I can't say I'm not disappointed," Maeve said. "But I meant everything I said. I want peace between us."

"The knight is still up at the castle, so we have to work together to figure out how to get rid of it," Sadie said.

"Do you know anyone who might know how to remove the curse?" C.J. asked Morag.

"Not a one," Morag said.

"What about Berwick?" Sadie asked.

"The owner of that bookstore?" Morag asked. "He sells some strange things in his shop, but as far as I know, he's just a shopkeeper. Some say he's related to the Romani Travelers, but I doubt it."

"Romani Travelers?" C.J. asked.

"Some called them Highland Gypsies," Morag said.

"Gypsies?" Sadie said. "They would know curses."

"That's just a myth," Morag told her. "The Romani are just normal people. They aren't magical."

"So, we can't remove the curse," Angus said. "What other choices do we still have?"

"What were you going to do with the knight once you had him chained up?" Quinn asked Greer.

"I thought I'd drop it into a Loch," Greer said, yawning. "Loch Domhain is just a couple of miles south of here. Maybe it would just sit at the bottom and rust."

"That sounds like a good idea," Scotty said. "We'd never see it again."

"It would return someday," Angus said. "The chains would rust before the armor does. It would just walk out of the lake once the chains rusted away."

"We certainly don't want to live under the shadow of it returning someday," Maeve said. "It might not come back in our lifetime, but I don't want it to hurt my future grandchildren or great-grandchildren, either."

Everyone fell silent.

"Can we just leave it where it is?" Scotty asked. "Just seal it up in the gatehouse?"

"We could," Quinn said. "But I think it would be like dropping it into the Loch. It's just a matter of time before it gets out. If you noticed, the castle is old, and some are crumbling. Eventually, no matter what we do, it will crumble away."

"We love our home," Maeve said, "but maintaining it is a lot of work. Sometimes it feels like it is crumbling down around us, even though most of it is still stable now."

"She's sleeping," Edna said, nodding toward Greer in the bed.

The doctor checked her. "She's fine. Why don't you all return to the waiting room and let her rest?"

Morag sat down in a chair near the bed. "I'm staying with her."

The rest filed out of the room and took their seats in the waiting room.

"You have a house in town here," Sadie said. "You can live there and visit the castle occasionally."

"Mollie and I could," Maeve said. "But it would still be too dangerous for Keir to go there."

"As long as the current Lord MacGregor doesn't return to the castle," C.J. said, "they will be safe. Everyone else has to leave the knight alone."

"That may be true," Angus said. "Though we don't know for sure it won't hurt anyone else, even if we leave it alone."

"But that's our ancestral home," Maeve said. "How would you feel if you couldn't ever return home?"

C.J. looked at his dad. "I have memories of Mom there," he said. "I wouldn't want to leave it."

"That's how we feel."

It was a long time before anyone spoke. C.J. moved to the window to think. He stared at the castle standing high on the hill above the town, visible above the nearby buildings.

He could also see the airship still moored beside it. It seemed long ago that they had come there. Now Keir's father was dead, and he couldn't return to his home.

They could all return to the airship and take off across the ocean, leaving the knight behind them. They wouldn't have to think about it again.

Sadie stood beside C.J. "What are you thinking about?"

"We could run away from all this, but Keir and his family can't do that. They can't run and hide. They must face up to the knight."

"I know. But what more can we do? We've done all we can. Or all we can think of, at least."

"We can't remove the curse," Scotty said. They looked up at him, suddenly standing over them. "And we can't physically destroy it."

"And if we imprison it," Sadie said. "It will just come back someday."

C.J. stared at the castle. "The knight was up there, waiting. And it will keep waiting until all the lords are dead or the walls crumble around it."

They all looked up at the castle. The sun was setting, and the shadows were gathering around the castle.

"The walls crumble down around it," C.J. repeated, looking down at the floor.

"We know," Sadie said.

"Yes," C.J. said. "That's what we need."

"What do we need?" Scotty asked.

"I think I know what we need to do." C.J. said, "But no one is going to like it." He looked back up at the castle. "No one is going to like it at all."

Chapter 50

"What are we not going to like?" Sadie asked.

C.J. returned to the adults. "I have a plan to get rid of the knight once and for all."

They looked at each other and then back at C.J.

"Ok," Angus said. "We're all ears."

C.J. spent the next several minutes explaining his plan and everyone's role. He could tell from their faces that there would be some serious objections, but he continued until it was done.

When he finished, there was utter silence in the room. It was so quiet that they could hear the few cars that passed the hospital outside.

Then, everyone talked all at once.

"That's far too dangerous," Angus said.

Maeve was adamant, "We can't risk Keir's life like that."

"There's so much that can go wrong with that," Walter said.

Edna held her hands up. "You could all get killed. I will not allow that."

C.J. stood silently, letting everyone put their objections on the table. He knew everyone would initially be emotional, and no one would listen until the shock had worn off.

"Laura will not take part in a stunt like that," Teresa said.

Jackson backed up his wife. "You are all too young to attempt something so dangerous."

C.J. waited until the conversation settled, and everyone began talking in groups of two or three. He raised his voice to be heard over all the conversations.

"I know that it's dangerous," he said and waited for everyone to quiet down. "I know. But we have little choice. We've talked about all the things we can try to do and tried all of them. None of them have worked." He looked around the room at all their faces. "It's the only way."

"It can't be the only way," Edna said. "There has to be a less dangerous way."

"Does anyone have any better ideas?" Sadie said. "We haven't been able to come up with any yet."

"Why don't you let us take care of it," Angus said. "It's too dangerous for you five."

"Keir needs to be part of it," C.J. said, "and we won't let him go through it alone. Besides, I didn't say no adults. This needs everyone to make it work."

"Why can't we wait and see if we can come up with something else?" Teresa asked.

"We talked about that too," C.J. said. "Any time we just wait, it puts the knight in control. It can bide its time until the advantage is his. We must take control and put the knight on the defensive."

Quinn, who had been silent to this point, spoke up. "He has a point. Instead of reacting to what the knight does, it is better to be proactive and make it do what we want."

"It's a gigantic risk," Maeve said. "I need to protect my son."

"Not doing anything is a risk, too," C.J. said. "And Keir is in danger as long as the knight is up there."

"He's just a boy," Maeve said.

"I know you're scared. And he's scared," C.J. said. "I'm scared too."

"And so are we," Sadie said, standing with Scotty and Laura.

"Even though he's just a boy and scared," C.J. said. "He is Lord MacGregor. He must take control of his castle and help us fight off this invader."

"And since he's the only one the knight is after, he's the only one that can lead it where we want it to go," Sadie added.

All eyes were on Keir. He was leaning against his mother. He looked up at her and then sat up straighter in his chair.

"I am scared," he said. "It's scary to have something out to kill you. I don't know if I can be brave enough."

"It's ok, Keir," his mother said to him.

Keir took a deep breath. "I don't know if I can be brave like you, but I'm tired of being scared all the time like this. Something must be done, and I'm the one that must do it."

"I just want to protect you," Maeve said.

"You can't protect me from the knight," Keir said. "If it wants to get me, there's nothing we can do about it. Maybe we can defeat it if we go after it."

"I still don't like it," Maeve said. "But you are the Lord of MacGregor Castle."

Keir straightened up a bit more in his chair.

"We'll all be with you," Angus said. The other adults nodded their agreement, some with some reservations.

"We have your back, young Lord," Quinn said and bowed to the boy.

"We will go to the castle in the morning," Maeve said.

"Yes," C.J. said. "We don't want to try this in the dark."

The following day, everyone gathered outside the castle's main gates to wait for the boy Lord to arrive at his castle.

The knight stood within the gatehouse, facing the drawbridge as if it were waiting for him to return as well.

Their car soon appeared on the road from town. Quinn slowly turned onto the drawbridge and crossed toward the castle. He stopped in front of the gate. The knight silently watched them.

"Are you ready?" Quinn asked Keir.

"As ready as I'll ever be," Keir said, looking ahead at the knight.

Quinn drove slowly around to the western gate and into the castle. The others followed them on foot.

When they arrived at the other side of the gatehouse, it startled everyone to see the knight was now facing the inside of the castle. It knew that Keir was there.

"Are you ready for this?" Maeve asked him. "We can go back to town if you're not."

Keir took a deep breath and let it out. "Let's do this."

Keir opened the car door and got out. He strode over to the gatehouse, trying to look and feel confident. He stopped, ensuring he was not within sword distance of the knight.

Summoning as much bravery as possible, he announced, "Lord MacGregor has returned!"

Chapter 51

The knight did not move. It stood facing the boy as if it were looking at him.

"Is this the first time it moved?" Quinn asked the guards.

"Yes, sir," one said. "It hadn't moved all day until the young Lord entered the castle."

The four kids walked up behind Keir and stood facing the knight. There was no sign the knight realized they were there or not. It didn't move even to adjust its stance.

Although his heart was pounding in his chest, Keir spoke again. "Did you hear me?" "I am the lord of this castle, and I have returned!" He waited for a response from the knight.

He took a step closer to the knight.

"Careful, Keir," Quinn said softly to him. "Don't get too close." He drew a line in front of the boy with the toe of his boot. "Don't go beyond this point."

Keir looked down at the line and took a half-step forward again, placing the toe of his shoes at Quinn's line.

Quinn nodded to the guard named Malcolm. He quickly disappeared up the steps to the room above the gatehouse.

The knight remained motionless.

Keir's mouth was dry. He knew the knight would make a move. The suspense was making him feel light-headed.

He placed one foot beyond the line and leaned in toward the knight. "This is my castle," he said. "I order you to leave it."

Malcolm returned carrying a halberd. He handed it to the other guard and ran back up the steps again.

The guard watched the knight carefully, holding the halberd at the ready.

Keir moved his back foot in front so that he was fully over the line Quinn had drawn in the dirt.

"Be ready," Quinn told him. He didn't take his eyes off the knight. He saw the knight's hand tightened on the sword hilt.

"Back!" he yelled, stretching his arm out in front of Keir to push him back behind the line.

The knight moved swiftly. It raised the sword and slipped it between the bars of the metal grating. Within seconds, he stabbed the sword at Keir, coming within inches of the boy's chest.

C.J. looked down at the line. Keir was standing just behind the line again.

The knight waved the sword from side to side, trying to reach the boy.

The guard brought the halberd down on the knight's arm. It caused the knight to drop the sword.

Before anyone could celebrate, the knight stuck its other arm through the grating and caught the falling sword. It withdrew the sword from the grating and stepped back from the portcullis.

It swiped the flat of the sword back and forth along the metal bands, causing the metal to ring painfully in everyone's ears.

The knight lunged toward the boy with the sword point again. When it missed, it withdrew again quickly to avoid being hit by the halberd.

It alternated between rattling the portcullis with the sword and lunging toward Keir for several minutes.

Each time it lunged, Keir would take a step back. But he would step back up to the line when it returned to rattling the bars.

No one knew how long it would keep up the pattern. But it came to a sudden stop when the portcullis raised a foot.

The knight stood without moving once again.

"Did we surprise it?" C.J. asked Quinn.

"Maybe," Quinn said. But to Keir, he said, "Don't let down your guard. He's ready to attack."

The knight sprang at the grating again. This time, it grabbed a crossbar with its free gauntlet and pulled up, trying to raise it some more.

The portcullis did not move.

The knight stabbed the sword down into the dirt. It stuck and wobbled back and forth. It grabbed the grating with both gauntleted hands and pulled up.

The portcullis rose an inch, but when the knight let go, it settled back down again.

Keir had moved one foot back, preparing to retreat if the knight had raised the grating. C.J. and the rest moved back and separated to avoid blocking Keir's retreat.

"Be ready to run," Quinn told the young Lord. "It is almost time."

The portcullis rose another half-foot.

The knight grabbed its sword, dropped to the ground next to the grating, and tried to slide under the bottom spikes. Although its arm and shoulder could fit through, the breastplate was too thick to get under it.

Everyone stepped back away from the struggling knight. Even as it tried to escape the gatehouse, it swung the sword toward anyone nearby.

The guard with the halberd kept trying to knock the sword from the knight's hand, but the knight was too quick for him.

"Are you ready to run?" Quinn asked Keir.

The boy didn't say a word. He just nodded as he stared at the cursed armor, trying to get out of its prison so it could kill him.

The knight swung the arm still trapped in the gatehouse at the grating and began pounding on it. The metal on metal rang loudly across the courtyard. Keir covered his ears with his hands.

"On your marks," Quinn said.

Keir and the other kids turned away from the knight but kept their eyes on it.

"Get set."

They hadn't run yet, but the anticipation had them breathing hard already.

With a screech, the portcullis rose another half-foot.

The knight slid under the grating. It was free.

"Go!" Quinn yelled.

The five kids took off across the courtyard toward the western side of the castle.

Quinn and the guard with the halberd moved to the side, away from the knight.

The knight stood with some difficulty. But once it was on its feet, it saw Keir running with the other kids around the corner of the castle.

It began running after them as fast as it could.

Chapter 52

The kids ran as fast as their legs would carry them. They listened for any sound, showing that the knight was catching up. But they heard nothing except their own pounding steps and heavy breathing.

They just hoped they could reach the garden before the knight caught up.

Keir fell behind the other kids. His lungs were straining to get a breath. He had never run this hard in his life.

They could see the entrance to the gardens ahead of them. If they could make it there, they would be safe.

Keir saw Scotty falling back, too.

C.J. glanced back at them. The knight turned the corner behind them and was running hard. "It's coming," he yelled. "Keep going. We're almost there."

Keir fell further behind. His breathing became ragged.

C.J. slowed down and grabbed his arm. Together, they ran harder toward the garden arches.

Laura and Sadie were far ahead of them. Scotty was running just behind C.J. and Keir. The knight was still behind them, but it was catching up fast.

Then everything turned upside down. Keir tripped over one of the many broken stones from the castle that littered the grounds. He went tumbling, pulling C.J. down with him.

They rolled on the ground, hitting several other stones until they came to a stop.

C.J. looked back. The knight was almost on them. He jumped back up on his feet and, with Scotty's help, dragged Keir to his feet as well. "Watch the stones," he warned Keir as they ran again.

Keir glanced over his shoulder at the knight.

"Don't look back," C.J. shouted at him. "Just run."

They reached the garden arches and ran through them into the castle's extensive gardens.

When they rounded the corner, they almost ran headlong into the group of castle men waiting in the garden for them.

Quinn stepped out in front of them and caught them as they were about to run by him. He brought them to a stop and directed them to the other side of the pit, where they found the knight. Laura, Sadie, and Scotty were already waiting there.

Quinn returned to where the men were and waited for the knight to race around the corner.

C.J. and Keir breathed heavily as they watched for the knight as well.

Several minutes went by. Everyone's attention was on the gate leading into the garden where the kids came through. But the knight didn't appear.

"Stay alert," Quinn told his men. "It has to be out there still."

"What's going on?" Keir asked in a whisper. "Where is it?"

"I don't know," C.J. said.

They saw the men looking around at each other.

"They're wondering where it is, too," Sadie said. "Did it know they were waiting for it?"

"How could it?" Scotty asked. "It's not psychic."

C.J. listened for a moment. "It's stopped. I can't hear it running."

He called to Quinn. "Is it just waiting out there?"

"Maybe," Quinn said. "I don't hear any movement."

"What do we do?" Sadie asked.

"I think Keir needs to let it know that he's still here," Quinn said. He glanced over at Keir. "Call out to it."

"What do I say?" he asked in a low voice.

"Anything," Quinn said. "You just have to make sure it knows you're still here."

Keir looked around at all the faces staring at him. He shrugged and called, "The Lord of the castle commands you to appear."

The knight did not appear. There was only silence.

"We need to get some eyes on the grounds out there," Quinn said. "Do I have any volunteers?"

The men began looking everywhere but at Quinn.

"Tavish," Quinn called. The man jumped. "Check it out."

Tavish looked wide-eyed at Quinn. "Yes, sir," he said reluctantly.

He left the ranks of the other men and stepped carefully toward the gate. Moving in a wide arc, he reached the archway on the opposite side from where the knight would come from.

He leaned forward to look along the wall, and after searching for any sign of the knight, he backed away until he was back with the other men.

He said with some relief, "The knight is gone."

"Are you certain?" Quinn asked him. "You looked everywhere?"

"Absolutely," Tavish said. "There was nowhere for it to hide out there. I could see the entire courtyard."

"Where could it have gone?" Keir asked. "It was right behind us."

Quinn began looking around the gardens and at the archways that surrounded it.

"It could come from anywhere," Quinn said. "Keep an eye out for any movement anywhere."

"Could it be in the garden already?" Keir asked, his eyes darting from one place to another.

"I don't think it is in the garden yet," Quinn said. "But it could come through any of those arches."

"Did it know we were waiting for it?" C.J. asked. "That it was walking into a trap?"

"Witchcraft," Scotty said. "The knight waited for you in the armor room upstairs. It just knows things."

"Let's not get carried away," Quinn said. "It's just tactics. It is probably just circling around to get ahead of you."

"Where is it then?" Keir said. "I don't like this."

"I don't like it either," Quinn said. "We just need to stay vigilant. It must be somewhere close."

Quinn joined the kids and watched the arches nearest them. He saw nothing out of the ordinary.

"What's that?" one man asked, pointing at a dark shape in one archway.

"It's just a bird," another man said.

"Stop jabbering," Quinn said, "and keep your eyes sharp. We don't want to be surprised."

Everyone fell silent.

Keir kept turning around, trying to look everywhere for the knight. C.J. put a hand on his shoulder. "Don't worry," he said. "Quinn knows what he's doing."

The sound of a twig snapping came from the archway nearest to Quinn and the kids.

And with only that warning, the knight dashed into the gardens.

Chapter 53

"The knight is here!" Quinn shouted to his men. He raised his rifle to shoot at the knight, but it was too close.

The kids scattered and ran through the gardens every which way. The knight turned to follow Keir.

Quinn stepped out in front of the knight. It swung its sword at him, but Quinn parried it with his rifle. The knight then pushed Quinn out of his way, sending him tumbling to the ground.

It continued past the prostrate Quinn and directly at Keir, who was fleeing toward the door into the castle.

He reached the door and pulled on it. It wouldn't budge. The door was locked.

Keir spun to the side just as the knight's sword slammed into the door and buried the blade several inches into the wood.

"Keir," C.J. called. "Get over here!"

Keir ran toward two of Quinn's men. After the boy had passed, they took their halberds and swung them both at the knight as it tried to run by.

The knight fell flat onto its back, but it immediately stood back up. The men backed away, out of the range of its sword.

Their blows did not stop the knight but slowed it down to give Keir time to get in position.

Keir saw a couple more men hiding behind a heavy stone balanced on the pit's edge. It was one of the stones set on top of the knight when the ancient lord buried it.

At the other end of the pit, C.J. and Sadie were standing on the edge of the pit with a rope dangling down into it. They were waving at him to run to them.

"You're almost there," C.J. yelled. "Jump into the pit."

When he glanced back, he saw the knight had just gotten to its feet and renewed the chase.

Keir took off toward the pit. A stack of stones stood between him and the nearest edge of the pit. He leaped up onto the lowest one and then leaped again.

After landing on the top stone, his foot slid on the crumbling surface. The boy skated across the stone and lunged off the edge to the ground below.

Behind him, the knight skirted around the stones and tried to intercept him.

Keir was almost at the pit when the knight rounded the stones.

"Jump," Sadie said. "Get into the pit!"

When he got to the edge of the pit, he paused for just a second, but when he heard the knight stomping up behind him, he leaped into the shallower end.

He fell to his knees but immediately tried to stand up. It was not the place he wanted to be. Behind him, the knight was approaching fast. Above him, the men were balancing the stone precariously.

He ran to the deeper end of the pit. The rope was waiting for him. He grabbed it with both hands and turned toward the knight.

The knight slid to a stop at the edge of the pit. It stood as if it were trying to decide what to do.

"Is it thinking?" C.J. whispered to the others.

Scotty nodded and said, "I told you. Witchcraft."

"The knight doesn't have a brain," Laura said. "It can't think."

"Maybe it's looking for some sort of opportunity," Sadie said. "Or a signal."

"Maybe Keir has to taunt him again," C.J. said. The others agreed.

"Keir," C.J. quietly called down to the boy in the pit.

Keir didn't respond. He stared at the knight at the other end of the pit.

"Keir," C.J. repeated. "Do you hear me?"

Keir slowly looked up at him.

"Call to it again," C.J. said. "Get it to climb down into the pit."

Keir's gaze went back to the knight. It still stood motionless at the edge of the pit as if it were waiting for a command.

"Climb down here." Keir tried to sound like it was a command, but his voice cracked. "Get into the pit," he added. "Now!"

The knight didn't move.

Keir dropped the rope and took a couple of steps toward the knight. "Did you hear me? Get down here!"

The knight tilted its head down as if looking into the pit.

Keir took a step back toward the rope.

The knight crouched down.

Keir backed to the end of the pit and grabbed the rope again. C.J. and Sadie prepared to haul him up.

The knight tried to balance on one bent leg and extended its other leg toward the pit. But when it began losing its balance, it pulled its leg back and stood up again.

"What are you waiting for?" Keir yelled.

The knight looked up at him and jumped down into the pit.

It stood at the end of the pit. The men behind the stone were ready, but the knight needed to be forward enough to be under it.

Keir wrapped the rope around himself and held onto it tight.

C.J. and Sadie were watching for the first movement of the knight to pull Keir up to safety.

Keir could barely breathe. He was alone in the pit with the knight trying to kill him.

"I'm right here!" Keir yelled. There was a note of panic in his voice. "Come get me!"

The knight took a step forward and then a second.

The men began pushing the stone over into the pit. Unfortunately, it was cumbersome, and leaning back against the wood logs holding it up. They pushed harder.

The knight took another step.

"Get me out of here," Keir yelled to C.J. and Sadie.

The knight picked up speed.

Then everything happened at once.

The knight's foot slid on some gravel at the bottom of the pit, causing him to tumble forward.

Keir closed his eyes as C.J. and Sadie pulled on the rope to get him out of the pit.

And the stone rocked as the men shoved it. Finally, it fell forward into the pit. The ground shook.

Chapter 54

When Keir opened his eyes, he was lying on the edge of the pit. He looked up at C.J. and Sadie.

"Did it work?" he asked. They didn't answer him, but stood staring into the pit.

When Keir stood up and looked down, he saw the knight sprawled on the ground at the deepest end of the pit. The stone fell in but missed the knight.

"Now, what do we do?" Keir asked.

C.J. and Sadie looked at each other. Sadie shrugged.

"We need to figure something out fast," C.J. said.

"You better," Keir said, looking back down at the knight.

The knight got up on its feet and bent down to pick up its sword. It looked up at Keir standing on the edge of the pit.

"What happened?" Keir asked.

"It didn't land in the right place," C.J. said. "They missed."

It reached up and swung the sword at Keir, but he and the other kids jumped back, away from the pit and out of range.

It sheathed its sword and grabbed the edge of the pit. Kicking its feet into the side, it climbed up and out.

Keir ran to the other side of the pit. The other kids scattered away from the knight in different directions.

When it stood on the edge, nobody was there to face him. It turned around, looking for Keir. When it spied him on the other side of the pit, it drew its sword and strode around the pit toward him.

Keir ran around the pile of stones and stood with the pile between him and the stalking knight.

The knight stopped when it reached the first stone. It looked at the pile of stones and then back at Keir. It then began making its way around the pile toward the boy.

Keir made his way along the pile of stones away from the knight, but the knight relentlessly followed him. He kept glancing around the garden, looking for the best way out.

Then he spotted it. There was a crawl space under several stones large enough for him to get into. He ran to it and ducked down to investigate. It created a tunnel from one end of the stone pile to the other.

Keir dived into the crawl space and headed to the other end. There wasn't enough room to look back at the way he'd come, so he kept crawling.

The tunnel was tight, and it felt like the stones were closing in on him. He focused on the light at the other end and crawled as fast as possible.

Then he heard a sound that made him freeze. It was thumping footsteps. The knight was running across the top of the stones. Dust and pebbles knocked loose by the vibration of the knight's steps pelted him. He coughed and wiped the dust out of his eyes.

The light at the other end darkened as the knight jumped off the stones and landed in front of it. It flattened itself on the ground and reached into the hole.

Keir slithered back along the tunnel. The knight's hand swiped at Keir's head, but only raked through his hair. Several hairs got caught in the joints of the metal hand and ripped out.

The knight tried to reach further into the tunnel, sliding its head under the stones to get a few extra inches, but Keir was far out of his reach.

Keir backed completely out of the tunnel. He stood up and looked around. The knight was on the far side of the stones, trying to extricate his head from the tunnel, but it was stuck.

Behind it was the pit. Scotty and Laura were on the other side while C.J. and Sadie were running toward them and waving.

It appeared they wanted him to jump over the pit. He would be jumping across the narrow part of the pit from where he was, but it still seemed too far to him.

The knight pulled its helmet from the tunnel with the screech of metal scraping on stone.

Keir asked himself what he was thinking as he leaped on the stone and ran toward the knight and the pit.

It freed itself from the tunnel and raised itself on its hands and knees.

Keir watched it rise as he ran toward it. He launched into the air, landed on the knight's back, slid to the ground behind him, and headed straight for the pit.

The knight turned in time to see him leap across the pit. He thought he was going to miss the other edge. But his foot caught it just enough to allow him to roll to the ground as the edge gave way under his foot.

The knight was on its feet instantly and running toward the pit.

"Get away from the pit!" Quinn yelled.

Scotty and C.J. grabbed Keir's arm and pulled him up off the ground, and then all five kids scattered.

The knight reached the edge of the pit and leaped across the hole toward them. It held its sword high above its head.

Quinn rushed forward and yelled to the kids again, "Get down on the ground!"

Coming to a stop, he dropped to one knee and raised his rifle to aim carefully at the knight.

The man seemed to wait forever to fire, and then there was a loud boom as he fired at the knight.

The knight seemed to stop mid-leap, but its sword flew out of its hand. It fell back and disappeared into the pit.

The blade arced end-over-end directly at the kids lying on the ground. Quinn could only watch in horror as the sword came down.

Chapter 55

The sword stabbed down into the ground just inches from Keir. It vibrated for a few seconds and then was still. Keir rolled away from it and stood up.

Quinn ran to the blade and pulled it out of the ground. It tugged at his hand, trying to move toward the pit and the knight at the bottom.

"What should we do?" Keir asked.

"Keep away from it," Quinn said. "And this sword, too."

The tugging was getting stronger. "Without the sword, he can't cut you, but he can still hit you with those metal gauntlets."

C.J. ran over to him. "Let's go through there," he said, pointing to the next set of archways. "We can hide in the bushes."

Keir wasn't listening to him. He was watching the hole. The knight had fallen in but hadn't reappeared. "Where is it?" he asked.

"It's down there," C.J. said. "Let's just go."

Keir edged closer to the pit, ignoring the warning from C.J. and Quinn.

"Listen to C.J.," Quinn yelled to him. Quinn was struggling while holding onto the sword. "Get out of here before it gets out."

C.J. grabbed Keir's arm and tried to pull him away, but Keir seemed mesmerized, trying to see what had happened to the knight.

"Keir!" Sadie called from the archways. "Get away from there!"

He had almost reached the edge of the pit when the knight stood up. The hole was shallow enough that its head and shoulders were above ground level.

Keir seemed to snap out of his trance and jumped back. The knight swiftly climbed out of the pit and stood over the boy. They could see that there were now two bullets embedded in its breastplate.

"Don't just stand there," Quinn called. "Run!"

Keir turned and ran with C.J. away from the knight and toward the archways.

But instead of following the boys, the knight headed straight for Quinn.

When Quinn saw the knight coming after him, he turned and ran for the back door. He thought about trying to shoot the knight again but had to hold on to the sword with both hands to control it.

When he got to the door, it wouldn't open. Quinn slammed the sword's pommel against the door several times, but then ran just before the knight caught up to him.

The knight stayed on his trail as he wound through the columns lining the garden.

The back door opened, and the Cook leaned out to see who was knocking at the entrance to the kitchen.

She saw Quinn with the knight in pursuit, and her eyes went wide.

"Hold the door open," Quinn yelled to her. He pretended to leave the garden through one archway, and when the knight tried to cut him off by going through a different archway, he ran back in and headed for the door and Cook.

"Be ready to shut the door behind me," Quinn called.

Cook pulled the door farther open and got out of his way just as he barreled through the doorway.

"Lock it!" he yelled.

Cook slammed the door, and the metal locking bar dropped into place. The knight ran full force into the door, but it held.

Quinn felt the sword lose some of its force, but it was still tugging toward its master. He ran down the hall and descended into the dungeon to secure the blade.

The knight continued to pound on the door, but the force of its blows lessened as the sword moved further out of its reach.

Once the knight gave up on retrieving its sword, it turned its attention back to Keir and headed past the pit and through the archways to the next garden.

It found itself on a path that wound through dozens of tall flowering bushes. It scanned the garden but could see none of the kids.

Moving along the path, first one way and then another, it wandered about the garden looking for any sign of Keir.

It sensed that the boy was somewhere in the garden but did not know where.

There was a rustling in a bush across the garden toward the outer wall. It ran along one path and then turned onto another when it veered away. When it reached the bush, there was no one there.

C.J. popped up from a bush toward the center of the garden. "Here I am," he called, dropping back into the bush again.

The knight ran toward that bush, straight through several bushes along the way. But when it arrived where the boy was, he was not there.

Laura popped up from a bush in a different part of the garden. "Hello," she said. "I'm over here."

The knight plowed through several bushes and headed straight toward Laura's hiding spot. But she was not there when it arrived.

The knight ripped every part of the bush from the ground, trying to find the girl.

Then it moved on to the next bush and ripped it all from the ground.

One bush after another, it moved through the garden, destroying the plant and then moving on to the next one.

Keir was hiding under a bush in the middle of the garden. By lying on the ground, he could see the feet of the knight as it moved through the garden.

He could also see where his friends were all hiding. They were slowly moving from one bush to the next on their way to the next set of archways and another garden farther on.

Keir was afraid to move. If he moved, he would make a noise and attract the knight's attention. He just stayed there under that bush.

The knight was getting closer. Soon it had ripped up a nearby plant and moved on to the one above him.

He could barely breathe when the knight stepped up and reached for the branches above him.

Chapter 56

As the branches ripped from the surrounding ground, Keir leaped to his feet and ran. He picked the wrong bush to hide under as the branches had thorns, and they caught at his clothes and skin as he pulled away from the knight.

The knight threw the branches away and chased after the boy.

The knight destroyed almost half the garden while searching for the young Lord, leaving Keir with little cover to hide.

He weaved through the remaining flowers, following one path and then another, heading toward where he had last seen the other kids.

The knight no longer followed the paths. It ran across paths and through bushes in his effort to follow the boy.

Keir glanced over his shoulder to see where the knight was as he zig-zagged through the garden. He was closing in on the archways, but at the same time, the knight was closing in on him. He wasn't sure that he was going to make it.

In his effort to monitor where the knight was, he wasn't watching the path ahead of him and tripped on a branch that had grown too far onto the path.

Keir fell face down onto the path and slid. Knowing the knight would be there in moments, he rolled toward the nearest shrub and crawled under it.

But he didn't stop there. He crawled from one bush to another, heading toward the last place he saw the other kids. At least, he hoped that was the direction. The boy feared he might have gotten turned around when he fell.

He crawled out of one shrub and crossed the path. Glancing around, he saw no sign of the knight. Diving under another plant, he kept going.

When he found himself hidden in the middle of three large bushes, he stopped and listened. The boy wasn't sure where he was in the garden and how much noise he had made while crawling.

He looked around and could see the columns of the archways just ahead of him. The gardener had been working by one column. A rake and a trellis leaned against the column, with several gardening tools scattered around the base.

Glancing around, he looked for the knight. But there was no sign of it. There was also no sign of the other kids.

Keir crawled back on the path and stood up. Getting ready to run, he glanced around the garden. He was alone.

He ran for the nearest arch that led to the next garden. Before he could get there, the knight stepped out from behind the column and blocked his way.

The knight tried to grab him, but he sidestepped it and ducked under his arms. He ran by the trellis and grabbed the rake around the column.

As he rounded the column, the knight met him on the other side. Keir swung the rake as hard as he could.

The rake connected with the knight's helmet, knocking it askew. It also caused the knight to stumble sideways a step.

The boy swung it back again. This time, he aimed at its leg. The head of the rake slammed into its knee and caused the knee to bend in the wrong direction.

The knight tried to take a step toward Keir, but the knee was stuck, and it almost lost its balance. As the knight attempted to straighten out its leg, Keir retreated.

He looked around the garden to see where he could go to get away from the knight, but there was no place to run. He was getting tired, and the knight would catch up to him soon.

The knight reappeared. It had fixed its knee and even straightened out its helmet. It ran straight for Keir.

Keir held the rake at the ready and swung it at the knight again when it closed in. The knight used its gauntleted hands to shield itself and deflected the rake away.

Keir's momentum caused him to spin around, and he lost his grip on the rake. It flew away and landed in a shrub.

As it approached, Keir fell onto his back and looked up at the knight. The knight lifted its leg and stomped down at Keir.

Keir rolled away as the foot came down heavily on the empty path. The boy jumped up and grabbed the rake out of the bush. He spun around to face the knight, swinging the rake as he turned.

The knight once again let the rake slam into its hands, but this time it held onto it and ripped it away from Keir. It broke the handle across its knee and threw the two halves down the pathway.

Keir took that opportunity to put some of the remaining bushes between him and the knight.

He glanced around the garden for an exit. He looked at the trellis leaning against the column and then up at the wall above the arches.

After getting rid of the rake, the knight turned and started wading through the shrubbery to get to Keir.

Keir took off around the bushes and ran straight at the column.

The knight tried to turn around while standing in the shrubbery, but the branches caught in the armor's joints slowed it down.

By the time the knight pulled itself free, Keir got to the trellis. He grabbed onto the crossbars and climbed them like it was a ladder.

When he reached the top of the trellis, he got his fingers on the edge of the wall above the arches and hung there briefly.

He saw the knight racing after him. Pulling himself up, he laid flat on his stomach, his legs dangling down.

Looking down, he watched as the knight began climbing the trellis. The boy swung one leg up onto the ledge.

Before he could swing his other leg up, the knight reached the top of the trellis and latched onto his ankle. When the knight pulled, he

felt the sharp edges of the armor slice into his foot, and he slipped off
the wall.

Chapter 57

Keir scrambled to stay on top of the ledge as the knight stood on the trellis, gripping his ankle. Keir's blood dripped down the column from the wound on his foot.

With each passing moment, Keir felt his grip on the edge of the wall slipping away. The knight had a firm hold on his ankle, and Keir knew that he only had a few seconds left before he would fall.

Keir kicked at the knight with his other foot to free himself, connecting with the thing's helmet. As the knight shifted its weight, Keir could hear a loud cracking sound.

The trellis gave way under the bulk of the knight, and its grip let loose as it fell back to the ground below.

Without hesitation, Keir pulled himself onto the ledge with his back to the upper wall and looked down at the knight. Blood still dripped from his injured foot, but he ignored the pain.

Keir watched as the knight lay motionless on the ground. He knew he hadn't defeated it, but something about how it lay there made him uneasy. It was too still, too silent.

Suddenly, the knight stirred and rose to its feet. Keir gasped in surprise. The visor of its helmet had broken off, revealing the emptiness inside. He knew no one was inside the armor, but seeing it move without a face sent shivers down his spine.

The knight's head looked up at Keir, and it lumbered toward the column below him.

It pounded on the column with both fists. Keir could feel the column vibrate and waver. The wall behind him rocked, sending pieces of masonry showering over him. A stone fell from the wall and landed on the ledge beside him.

When he turned to look where it came from, he found a hole in the wall. He could see through it to the other garden behind him. His four friends were standing below him on the upper part of the wall that had almost fallen on C.J. so long ago, it seemed.

Keir knew if he wanted to stay on the ledge, he had to act fast.

He grabbed the stone from the ledge and hurled it down onto the knight with all his might.

The stone struck the knight on the shoulder just as it was about to pound the column again.

It staggered backward and looked back up at the boy.

Keir imagined the invisible face inside the helmet was turning red with rage, and although it made no noise, he could almost hear it roaring its anger at him.

He turned to the hole in the wall again.

"Throw stones at him," he yelled to the kids below. "It will keep it busy."

The kids hesitated for a moment. But the urgency in Keir's voice was enough to spur them into action. They picked up stones and threw them at the knight one by one. The rocks bounced harmlessly off the armor, but the knight still flinched at each impact.

Keir watched as the knight charged at the kids.

As the four of them ran frantically through the garden, the knight chased after them.

Laura stumbled and fell to the ground. The knight approached her as she scooted backward away from him.

As it reached out to grab her, something unexpected happened. A stone slammed into the side of the knight's helmet, causing it to stumble to the side. It glanced to see where the stone had come from and found Scotty standing defiantly nearby.

C.J. and Sadie cheered as Laura leaped up and ran away while the knight faced down the boy.

Scotty laughed for a moment before he realized the position he was in. As the knight began advancing, the boy ran for his life.

With no more kids challenging him, the knight returned to the column and the boy, who was just out of his reach.

It looked at the pile of broken boards that had recently been a trellis. That would no longer help him climb up to get to the boy.

The knight circled the column, looking for another way to climb up or bring the boy down. It stopped to look at the fallen wall. If it stood on the wall, it would still be nowhere near high enough to reach the ledge above.

The knight skirted around the fallen wall and continued around the column. When it was back by the trellis, it picked up several of the wooden slats and looked up at Keir.

It whipped the slats at him one at a time.

Keir tried to dodge the boards, but two of them hit him. One caught his shoulder, and the other landed squarely in his chest. It knocked the breath out of him, but he stayed standing. When the knight bent down to gather more slats, Keir made his way along the ledge to where a section of wall had fallen years before.

He stepped around it to the ledge on the other side.

When the knight had gathered the slats, it looked up to find Keir was gone. It hurried through the archway to the other side and found him on the ledge.

It again threw the slats at the boy. Most of them missed, but one hit him on the back.

Pain shot through Keir, and he found it hard to breathe again. He clutched the wall to steady himself.

The knight stepped up to the column, slammed its fists onto it, and then backed up to see if the boy would fall.

The column rocked again. Already barely able to stand, Keir stumbled on the ledge and searched the wall for a handhold to catch himself.

The wall itself rocked along with the column. Keir slipped down and fell flat on the narrow ledge. Before he knew it, he felt himself slipping off the edge.

Chapter 58

Keir scrambled to find something to hold onto. His fingertips grazed the rough surface of the stone but couldn't find a secure grip. Panic set in as he felt his body slipping further off the ledge.

Suddenly, his hand found a protruding edge. He grabbed it and held on with all his might. His legs swung precariously, but he found another hold, then another. He clung to the ledge, panting, trying to calm his racing heart.

As he looked down, he saw the long drop below him, and his stomach churned. His mind raced with thoughts of what could have happened if he had fallen, broken bones, or worse, death at the hands of the knight.

The swaying of the old stone column finally stopped. Peering down, he saw the armored knight standing below him. He wondered how long he would be stuck up on that ledge.

Keir glanced around the garden. The four kids hid among the flowers in the garden, scattered throughout the garden. Quinn was also nowhere to be seen. He hoped the sword hadn't injured the man.

The knight moved to the column again. Keir grabbed onto whatever handholds he could find to prepare for the impact. He closed his eyes in anticipation.

But no impact came. He looked down again and saw the knight reaching up and running its gauntlets across the stone surface.

Suddenly, Keir realized what it was doing.

"It wants to climb up here," Keir yelled to the other kids.

They popped out of their hiding places to see what the knight was doing.

Once it found a couple of handholds, it tentatively tried a step and lifted itself onto the wall. One step at a time, it moved up the wall toward Keir.

Keir yelled down, "Try to knock him off the wall."

The kids sprang into action. They ran to pick up stones, sticks, or anything else heavy enough to throw at the knight.

Sadie was the first to get into position. She launched two stones in quick succession at the back of the knight. One caught him on its shoulder, and the other hit a leg.

The knight paused for a moment but continued as the stones fell to the ground below it.

Scotty was next. After Sadie retrieved her stones, he threw one at the knight's head. The rock missed and hit the wall just above him. His disappointment lasted just an instant as the rock fell on top of the knight's helmet.

It didn't hit hard, but it was just enough distraction to cause one of his feet to lose its toehold. The knight slid down as its weight shifted to the foot that still had a good hold. After it stabilized itself, it tried climbing again.

C.J. hurled a couple of stones at the knight. They both hit the knight, one on its left knee and the other on its right foot. But neither one slowed it down.

When Laura called out to her, Sadie was about to take another turn throwing stones at it.

"Wait a minute. Give me a chance," she said, holding out the lower half of the rake.

Sadie backed up and let her at the knight.

She rushed over to the column and stood below the knight. Holding the rake up, she tried to hook one of its feet with the rake's head, but the knight was just out of reach.

Sadie hopped onto the fallen wall and tried again. She hooked it around one of its legs and pulled back. It didn't budge until she pulled again with all her might. The foot came loose, and the knight dropped until both arms were outstretched.

She spun around and whacked the rake on the side of its other leg. The rake barely hooked its other foot. Pulling with all her might, she yanked on that foot. It slid out of its toehold.

She fell backward onto the fallen wall. The rake clattering away somewhere into the garden. She looked up and watched the knight scrape at the wall with its feet, almost like it was trying to run up the wall.

But it wasn't able to get a new toehold. It fell backward off the wall. Laura rolled off the fallen wall just before the knight slammed into it.

The kids scattered before the knight could recover and stand up again.

Keir looked down at the knight lying on the wall that had almost killed C.J. when he had first arrived.

His eyes widened, and he jumped up and stood on the ledge. He hurried down the wall again and around to the opposite side.

"Try to keep him there," he yelled. "Don't let him stand up."

The other kids watched the knight get up.

"How do we do that?" C.J. yelled back.

Keir moved along the wall, back to the middle again. "I don't know," he yelled down through the small hole in the wall. "Hit him again!"

He put his hands on the wall and pressed lightly. The wall seemed solid. Pushing harder on it, he felt it give a little. But he also felt his balance shifting to where he could fall backward off the wall.

He looked back through the hole and saw the knight climbing off the fallen wall.

C.J. and Sadie were throwing rocks at the knight. Although they slowed it down, it quickly got off the wall. Once it stood up, it caught one stone and threw it back at the boy. He barely ducked down in time. He felt it rush by his head and heard it skip across the pathway behind him.

After retrieving the rake, Laura snuck up behind him and swung it at its helmet. The knight seemed to know she was there and raised its hand to intercept the rake. It grabbed and pulled on it, causing the girl to tumble onto the pathway beside it. She jumped up and ran as it lobbed the rake to a distant part of the garden.

After the kids left it alone, it returned to the column and slammed its fists against it again.

Keir felt the impact and watched the wall rock back and forth. He grabbed onto it to steady both himself and the wall.

He hoped the wall wouldn't fall too soon. And that it wouldn't take him with it.

Chapter 59

After locking the sword in the hidden room where Greer had originally stashed the armor, Quinn returned from the dungeon. He convinced Cook to close the door behind him and rushed into the gardens again.

He heard the door close and latched as he glanced around the yard. It was empty. There was no sign of the knight, the kids, or his men.

"Where'd they all go?" he asked himself.

He heard a commotion on the other side of the archways, so he ran to the next garden. He came to a stop when he saw the devastation in that garden.

"What the devil happened here?" he asked himself again. He glanced around and spotted Keir flailing around on top of one column. Quinn dashed across the garden to the base of the column.

"What's happening, Keir?" Quinn shouted at him.

The boy steadied himself and looked down to see the knight circling the column, heading for Quinn's position.

"Watch out!" Keir called down. "The knight's right there!" He pointed just in time for Quinn to see it step out from behind the column.

Quinn turned and ran around to the other side of the column. When the knight didn't follow, he knew the knight wasn't after him.

"Can you hear me, Keir?" he yelled up to him.

He couldn't see the boy behind the wall but heard his "Yes" call back.

"Where are the other kids?"

"We're right here," C.J. said, popping up from the flowers behind him.

Quinn spun around and saw all four emerging from their hiding spots.

"Are you all ok?" he asked.

"We're good," Sadie told him. "But the knight has almost knocked Keir off that wall."

"Where are my men?" Quinn asked, looking around the garden.

"We don't know," C.J. said. "We haven't seen them in a while."

"Why would they just leave you like that?" Quinn growled.

"Don't worry about that right now. There are more urgent problems," Sadie said. "We need to get the knight on that fallen wall."

Quinn glanced at the wall. "On that? Why?"

"The stonework is loose," C.J. said, pointing at the wall on top of the column. "Keir wants to push it over onto the knight."

"What's that going to do?" Quinn asked.

"Hopefully, it will crush it," Scotty said.

"But we couldn't crush it."

"Not with a hammer," Laura said. "But a ton of stone landing on it? That should do some damage."

Quinn looked up at the upper wall. "Maybe," he said. "But what if it doesn't work?"

"Do you have any other ideas?" Sadie asked. "If we don't do something soon, Keir will fall from up there."

"We need to get it back over here," C.J. said.

Quinn unslung his rifle. "Leave it to me," he said and rushed to the other side of the column.

He found the knight trying to climb up the side of the column.

"Oh, no, you don't," Quinn said. He jabbed the butt of the rifle at the knight.

It whirled on him and swung its fists. Quinn ducked back, and when he saw another opening, he jabbed at him again.

He continued ducking the knight's swings and jabbing at him while leading it around the column to the stone slab on the other side.

The knight swung at Quinn again. But, when the man tried to jab him again, the Knight grabbed the rifle out of his hands and flung it across the slab. Quinn watched it sail off into some bushes.

When he looked back at the Knight, its fists were closing in on his head. He dropped to one knee. After hearing them crash together above him, he launched himself onto the slab and rolled across to the other side.

When the knight turned away to return to the column, C.J. jumped onto the slab with a fist full of small rocks. He threw one of them at the knight. It bounced off its breastplate.

"Do you like that?" C.J. asked it. He threw another rock at its head.

The knight stepped forward so that its shins were up against the slab and tried to grab the boy.

C.J. danced around out of its reach and threw another stone at it.

When Keir saw the knight next to the slab, he slowly made his way along the ledge to another wall above where the knight was standing.

There were no holes in that wall that he could use to aim, so he just had to rely on luck. Keir pushed against the wall, but it didn't give way. He pressed harder against it, but it was solid.

Laughing to himself, he never thought it would disappoint him that part of the castle would not fall apart.

Making his way back to the loose wall section, He looked down through the hole and saw the knight standing next to the slab.

C.J. was weaving around and taunting it, but the knight was not attempting to climb onto it.

"Get the knight up on the slab," Keir yelled.

Quinn finally located his rifle and aimed it at the knight. It was on the wrong side of the slab, so shooting it would do no good. Besides, C.J. was bouncing in and out of the shot. He lowered the rifle.

"C.J., get out of there," Quinn yelled to him.

C.J. glanced back at Quinn, taking his attention away from the knight for a second. The knight took advantage of that and grabbed the boy by his shirt and lifted him off the ground.

Quinn raised his rifle again, but the knight held C.J. in front of him, so he didn't have a good shot. He might have hit the boy.

If they didn't do something quickly, the knight might kill C.J.

Chapter 60

The knight held C.J. until they were face to helmet. C.J. almost expected to smell the knight's foul breath, but it just smelled earthy from being buried for so many years.

It slowly raised its other hand to C.J., wrapping the metal fingers around his throat. It squeezed.

C.J. saw a blur behind the knight. He wasn't sure whether it was real or just an apparition created by his brain getting low on oxygen.

But then, something passed before his eyes and slammed into the knight's hands. He felt himself falling away from the knight and landing on his back on the ground.

As the oxygen flowed back into his brain, he saw Greer holding a halberd. She was facing down the knight, although they were both upside down from C.J.'s perspective.

"You thought you'd have all the fun?" she asked the boy. "You can't leave me out of this."

She pummeled the knight with the halberd again, causing it to back up away from the slab of stone.

"Greer! Get him up on the stone slab," Sadie yelled. "Don't force it away!"

"On the slab?" she asked, glancing behind her for a second. "What's that going to do?"

"Keir's going to drop a wall on it," Scotty shouted.

Greer let up on her attack and ducked under its arm when it tried to swing at her. She got behind it and whacked it with the halberd.

It spun around and tried to swing at her again. Greer did a double take. One of its gauntlets was missing.

"Where did its hand go?" Greer asked loud enough for the other kids to hear.

C.J. had just stood up. When he looked down, he saw the gauntlet still clutching his shirt. He let out a yell and tried to knock it off.

The hand twisted at his shirt. He grabbed onto it and tried to disentangle it from his clothes. As fast as he untwisted it, it would dig in further.

Finally, he yanked the gauntlet as hard as he could, his shirt ripped, and the hand came free, still holding part of his collar.

"Ew," he said. "I've got his hand."

The knight turned toward the boy and glanced at his arm where the gauntlet was missing.

Greer continued to wallop it with the halberd, but the knight focused on getting its hand back.

C.J. held onto the gauntlet and ran.

The knight chased him through the garden and around the columns surrounding it. He concentrated more on holding the gauntlet so that its grasping fingers didn't get a hold of him than where he was going.

"C.J., you're running the wrong way!" Sadie yelled at him. "You need to bring him back to the slab!"

He glanced around to see where he was and realized Sadie was right. He was leading the knight away from where they wanted it.

C.J. circled back around some bushes and headed back to the slab. The knight cut through the plants to get at the boy and his hand, but C.J. was quicker and stayed ahead.

When he returned to the fallen wall, Greer was still there, ready with the halberd.

"Stand back," C.J. told her. "Let it come after me."

The girl nodded and retreated.

C.J. leaped onto the slab and waved the gauntlet around. "Do you want this?" he asked it.

The knight stopped at the edge of the fallen wall.

As C.J. moved the hand, the knight's gaze followed it. He began dancing around, shifting it from one side to the other.

"If you want it," C.J. said, "you have to come get it."

He backed up, giving the knight plenty of space to climb onto the slab. But the knight made no move to climb up.

He held the gauntlet out to the knight. "Don't you want it?" He looked at the fingers curling and uncurling repeatedly. He wrinkled his nose at it. "I certainly don't want it."

He looked back at the knight, still motionless.

"Come on," C.J. yelled at it. "What must I do to get you to come after it?"

The knight suddenly lurched.

It startled C.J. He instinctively jumped and stepped away from the knight. But his foot only found air behind him. Without realizing it, he was already at the far edge of the slab. He tumbled backward and landed flat on his back. Again.

The knight swiftly moved around the slab to get to C.J. and the gauntlet.

C.J. looked around but didn't see the hand anywhere.

He dropped it as he fell and didn't know where it fell.

He quickly gave up the search when the knight rounded the end of the slab and backed away.

When the knight realized C.J. no longer had the gauntlet, it ignored the boy and glanced around for it.

They both saw it at the same time. The hand slowly crawled across the garden path, trying to return to the knight.

It took a step toward the gauntlet when C.J. heard Quinn.

"Drop to the ground," Quinn yelled. "Now!"

Without thinking, C.J. obeyed. He dropped to the ground and covered his head.

Quinn had his rifle raised and had the knight in his sight. The crack of the shot rang out in the enclosed garden.

C.J. looked up at the knight. It had fallen back into a sitting position on the edge of the slab, the third bullet joining the first two in its chest.

It stood up again. C.J. heard a click and jumped up to see Quinn checking his rifle.

He turned back to the knight. It was standing up again and off the stone.

"C.J., take this," Greer yelled.

He looked to where Greer was standing. She held the halberd and threw it toward him.

He grabbed it out of the air and aimed it at the knight. He ran full bore at it.

It connected with its breastplate and knocked it back onto the slab.

He cheered but stopped short when he felt himself being pulled onto the slab, too. The knight had grabbed the halberd and pulled it. And C.J. went with it.

When he landed on the stones, he saw the wall on the ledge rock. He released the halberd and let himself roll to the other side of the slab and tumble off the edge.

He jumped up and backed away. The knight sat up and turned its head to look at him.

Then the other part of the wall came down on it. C.J. saw the helmet crumple down into the breastplate. Then the rest of the knight flattened under the immense weight of the stone wall.

He heard everyone cheering and was about to cheer with them when he looked up. There was no sign of Keir on the ledge above.

Chapter 61

"Where's Keir," C.J. called. "He's not up there."

Quinn ran to the fallen wall to see if Keir had fallen with it. But he wasn't anywhere around it.

Keir's voice called to them. "I need some help here."

Quinn went around to the other side of the column. He found Keir hanging from the ledge by his fingers.

"I can't hang on much longer," Keir yelled.

Quinn dropped his rifle and stood at the bottom of the column. "Let yourself go," he told the boy. "I'll catch you."

"Are you sure?"

"Yes, I've got you."

Keir let himself fall. Quinn didn't catch him as much as he broke the boy's fall. They both fell back onto the garden path.

"Are you all right?" Quinn asked as the boy rolled off him.

"I think so. How about you?"

Quinn stood up and stretched his back. "I've been worse."

"Did it crush it?" Keir asked as he, too, stood up.

"It looked like it. I'll have to find where my men disappeared and get them to help look at it."

The other kids rushed in and surrounded Keir. They all fired questions at him. He just held up his hands and smiled.

"You did it," C.J. told him. "It landed right on it. I saw it crumple up."

"Really?" Keir asked. "Is it... dead?"

"I think so."

Maeve practically flew across the garden as she rushed over to her son. She grabbed him by the shoulders and checked him for any injuries. Except for the cuts on his ankle, she found none. She pulled him into a hug.

"I'm so glad you're ok," she told him. "I'm incredibly proud of you."

The other parents arrived shortly after Maeve and had their reunions with their kids, too. The same conversations played out, with each expressing their relief and pride, as well as giving their kids fierce hugs.

They spent some time in the garden as the kids told their parents what they had done to help fight the knight.

"The original plan didn't work out," C.J. said. "But Keir figured out a different way to do it."

"I don't know if we would have been able to destroy it if it weren't for Keir," Sadie told Maeve.

Scotty and Laura agreed with Sadie.

"Greer helped too," C.J. said, spotting the girl standing away from the group.

Maeve looked around, and when she saw the girl, she called her over. Greer stood in front of the woman with her eyes on the ground.

Maeve gathered the girl into a hug. Greer stood stiffly in her arms. "Thank you for helping set things right."

Greer relaxed and hugged her back. "I did what I could. But Keir is the one who defeated it."

Maeve went back to hugging Keir.

"Is it defeated?" Maeve asked Quinn. "Is the curse broken?"

"I don't know," Quinn said. "I'll try to get some men to come out here and check it out."

Maeve nodded, and Quinn went back into the castle.

Angus noticed C.J.'s torn shirt. "What happened to your shirt?"

"The knight grabbed me," his son told him. "Greer knocked its hand off, but it kept holding onto me. I had to rip it off."

"Where did that hand go?" Greer asked.

The kids went back to search for the hand, but after many minutes of searching, they couldn't locate it.

They finally called off the search when Quinn returned with several of his men.

"They aren't the ones who helped us earlier," C.J. whispered to Sadie.

"I don't think Quinn is thrilled with the other ones," Sadie said.

Quinn had them surround the fallen wall. Each man held a large crowbar and searched for a place to get some leverage.

"Should we just leave the stone?" Maeve asked. "What if it's still under there, just waiting?"

"Do you want us to leave it there?" Quinn asked. "If it is just waiting, it might surprise us one day."

"I want to know for sure," Keir said. "I want you to remove the stones."

Quinn looked at him and said thoughtfully, "Yes, M'Lord."

He gave the command to break the fallen wall apart.

The men began prying off piece after piece of the slab. As they pried a chunk off, the kids helped to carry the pieces off. They found an open area where they could pile them up.

As the day dragged on, the pile got larger.

When one man took a break, Scotty picked up his crowbar to break off a few small pieces of stone. When the man returned to work, Scotty was glad to let him have his crowbar back.

"My back hurts," he complained to his sister.

Sadie smiled at him as she grabbed more broken stones to carry to the pile.

Then one man called out. "I found some metal."

Everyone rushed over to where he was working to look at the slab. A small piece of metal stuck out from between the layers of stone. It looked like a piece of armor, although no one knew which part it was.

But they were all sure that the wall had crushed it flat.

They continued to pry apart the wall, concentrating on the area around the piece of metal they found.

They uncovered more and more of the armor, and from what they found, it seemed that the knight had been flattened.

With renewed effort, they broke apart the rest of the wall until they had uncovered the entire piece of metal that had just recently been an animated suit of armor.

But it wasn't anymore. The stone wall had crushed and folded the knight into a flattened blob of inanimate metal.

"Keir killed it!" Scotty said.

"It wasn't alive," his father told him. "But I agree. Keir killed it!"

While everyone celebrated the end of the knight and its reign of terror, C.J. stared at one flattened arm that stuck out from the rest of the mass. The one arm without a gauntlet.

Chapter 62

With the end of the knight, life at the castle became less distressing, but not quite happier yet. Without the danger of the knight to worry about, Maeve and her kids could start grieving over the loss of Alastair.

A few days later, Angus and the other adults decided it was time for them to head back across the ocean and back to their own homes.

"We were just enjoying the castle," C.J. said. "And now we have to go?"

"We've already been here longer than we'd planned," his father told him. "It's time for us to head back home."

"What about Keir and Mollie?" Sadie asked. "They just lost their dad. They need us here."

"I'm sure they are glad you're here," Sadie's father told her. "But they need time on their own too."

"We can come back and visit in the future," Edna said. "Hopefully, that will be a more enjoyable visit."

C.J. was about to object again, but his father ended the conversation. "You have the rest of tonight," he said. "We will get ready to leave in the morning."

They spent the evening with Keir and Mollie, playing games and finally getting an official tour of the castle, including areas they hadn't seen during their recent adventures.

The following day, after breakfast, they packed their bags and took one last look around their rooms before bringing their luggage down to the front hall. Their parents had already brought their luggage down, so they added it to the pile.

Quinn was there directing some men to load it all up in a truck waiting outside to cart it around to the airship sitting outside the walls.

As the men hauled the bags out through the doors, Morag and Greer passed them coming in.

"I heard you're all leaving," Greer said.

"Yeah," C.J. said. "We have to go home."

"I just wanted to catch you before you go," Greer said. "I wanted to thank you, all of you." She looked around at all the kids. "If it weren't for you, my grandmother and I would have wasted the rest of our lives hating the MacGregors."

"It's like a weight has been lifted off me," Morag said. "I was so focused on hate. I wasted the time I had with Greer. Now, I plan on enjoying my time with her."

Greer smiled at her and hugged her.

"We're glad," Sadie said. She gave Greer a sharp look. "We heard you snuck out of the hospital the other day."

Greer blushed. "I wanted to help, and they wouldn't let me leave."

"Are you ok?" Laura asked.

"I am now. But I will not mess with any more knights in the future."

"You have a safe trip home," Morag told them. "Though I don't know why anyone would want to go up in the sky in that thing."

"You should try it sometime," Scotty said. "It's great to look down at all the tiny houses."

"I'll keep my feet on solid ground, if you don't mind," Morag said.

After they said their goodbyes, Greer and Morag headed back home.

As they left, Maeve and her kids entered the front hall. Quinn and the kids' parents joined them.

"Was that Morag?" Maeve asked.

"They just wanted to say goodbye," Sadie told her. "It looks like they really are giving up their animosity toward us MacGregors."

"I'm glad to hear that," Maeve said. "I'll have to invite them up here."

She asked the kids to gather around her. Quinn handed her some pins.

"Alastair designed these simple medals. He wanted to honor veterans from the area who served in the great war. You four have earned them for protecting the Lord of Castle MacGregor."

She pinned one on each of the four Young Explorers.

"These designate you all honorary knights. I thank you for helping protect Keir and destroying the cursed knight."

"Even Sadie and Laura?" Scotty asked.

"Haven't you heard?" Maeve asked. "Women can be knighted too these days."

"Congratulations," Angus said to all of them. The other parents congratulated them, too.

The four kids looked at their medals and couldn't help but smile.

Mollie hugged each one, from C.J. to Sadie and Scotty to Laura.

"Thank you for saving my brother," she told them. She dropped her voice. "He can be a jerk sometimes, but he's still my brother."

"Hey!" Keir said. "Remember, I'm the Lord here."

"How can anyone forget," Mollie said. "You keep reminding us."

"Let's all be civil," Maeve reminded them. "Besides, you're still a Lord-in-training until you are 18."

Quinn's men packed the last luggage into the truck and headed to the airship. A car drove up to chauffeur the adults while the kids wanted to walk out to the airship.

"You are all welcome to return anytime," Maeve told them.

Everyone thanked her. Edna and Walter hugged her goodbye and followed the rest to the car.

Mollie and Keir walked with the rest of the kids as they crossed the courtyard and left the castle for the last time.

When they arrived at the airship, the engines were already going.

The stewards were loading the last of the luggage from the truck up the ramp and into the guest quarters.

Angus and Jackson were talking with the pilots.

"I guess this is it," Scotty said, looking up at the castle towering over them. "I am going to miss your castle."

"Well, I'm going to miss both of you," Sadie said, giving both Keir and Mollie hugs.

Scotty blushed, "I'm going to miss them too."

Quinn walked over to the kids and shook each of their hands.

"It has been a pleasure to have you visit," he told them. "You have shown your bravery and loyalty well. You well deserve those medals." He bowed to them all before they went to board the airship.

As they climbed the stairs to the gondola, Scotty looked at the medal again. "Do you think we could be knights?"

"I think so," C.J. said. "But I'm staying away from any kind of armored knights."

"You never know what we may run into," Sadie said.

"Well, no Scottish Knights anyway," C.J. said.

Chapter 63

As soon as the passengers boarded, the crew pulled up the steps and secured the door.

Everyone walked along the corridor inside the airship and up to the second level. They spread out around the observation deck.

The adults broke up into small groups to talk or work on recording what they had experienced in Scotland.

The kids took places near the windows to look at the scenery. They kneeled on the seats, leaning out the windows and looking at the ground.

Below them, a lot of activity was taking place.

Quinn's men untied each tether, freeing the airship from the ground. As it floated slowly upward, the crew pulled the lines in and prepared the gondola for the flight across the ocean back to the United States.

Just before getting into the car to return to the castle, Quinn glanced up at the airship. Seeing the kids looking out, he waved to them.

They all waved back until he ducked down into the car.

The airship continued to float upward until it was above the outside walls of the castle. They could hear the crew revving up the engines as it climbed even higher. The ship turned slowly away from the castle and toward the town below it.

As it drifted off the hill that had been its home for many days, the airship passed over the moat surrounding the castle and began a grand circle tour of the town.

When they arrived in Scotland, they had passed over the town, but this time, they were more familiar with some corners of the little village.

"There's Berwick's," Sadie called out, pointing at the little curiosity shop they had visited and where they had found the book on curses.

As they floated above the church at the center of town, Scotty pointed out the hospital behind it.

"That's one place I want to avoid when we come back," Scotty said. The others agreed with him. Most of them had seen the inside of a hospital more on this trip than at any other time in their brief lives.

C.J. thought about his mother. He had not been a fan of hospitals even before this trip. The last time he'd seen her, she was so frail in her hospital bed.

Sadie began waving to someone out of the window. C.J. looked down and saw Morag's house looking small below them. Both Morag and Greer were out in the yard, waving up.

He joined the others in waving back at them.

As the airship turned back toward the castle, the pair stood out in their yard, watching them fly away. Soon, the grandmother and granddaughter were out of sight behind them.

While flying over the town, they had gained enough height that they were well above the castle. They flew above it one last time before heading off to the coast.

They recognized two tiny figures in the courtyard waving at them. It was Mollie and Keir. They leaned out the windows to wave down at them.

"Careful," Edna called out to them. "Don't lean out so far."

They continued to wave until those figures disappeared behind them as well. When no one remained to wave to, they sat back in their seats.

Soon the airship left MacGregor Castle and the town of Oorlich far behind them.

While some adults talked quietly among themselves, the four kids sat without talking. Some stared out of the windows at the countryside rolling by while the others contemplated what had happened to them while visiting the castle.

After a couple of hours, C.J. caught sight of the ocean. He watched as the coast of Scotland slipped slowly and silently out from beneath them. Soon there was nothing to see except water from horizon to horizon.

Angus broke the silence by clearing his throat. "I think it is time, don't you think?" he asked Edna.

"Yes," Edna replied. "I believe so."

"Time for what?" Sadie asked.

"You'll see," Edna said as Angus and Walter stood up and left the room.

Chapter 64

"What's going on?" Scotty asked. "Where did Dad go?"

"They just went to get a few things," Edna told them.

"What things?" C.J. asked.

Edna just smiled at them. "You'll see in good time."

When they returned, each of the men carried a couple of boxes. They placed them on the table in the center of the observation deck.

"What are those?" Sadie asked.

"Be patient," her mother told her.

"We are all very proud of every one of you," Angus said.

"When you told us your plan for the knight," Edna said, "we weren't, shall we say, enthusiastic about it."

"I didn't like it at all," Walter said, folding his arms in front of him.

"Yes," Angus said. "But we were out of ideas. So, we went with your plan."

"On the condition that Quinn and his men were with you," Teresa added.

"Quinn's men didn't stay with us," Scotty said.

Sadie elbowed him.

"They stayed in the beginning, at least," Scotty said.

"Anyway," Edna said. "Everything worked out in the end."

"We wanted to commemorate this trip by giving you some souvenirs we brought back," Angus said.

Angus nodded to Teresa.

"Laura," she called. "What is something that stood out about this trip for you?"

Laura thought about it for a moment. "I guess I was excited about removing the curse."

"You were," Teresa said.

"Yes, when we found the book, I thought we could remove it with that spell. I was so disappointed that I failed."

"You learned Gaelic on the way here and used it to help the entire time we were at the castle, and you thought you failed?" her mother asked.

"Well, yes. I found the spell and cast it. It failed because of me," Laura said.

"Not everything in life works," Teresa told her. "You only fail if you stop trying. You kept trying until you succeeded, just with a different plan."

She stood up and took one box from the table. She handed it to Laura and stood back, waiting for her to open it.

Laura set the box on her lap and just looked at it.

"Are you going to open it?" her mother asked.

She took a deep breath, opened the lid, and looked into the box.

After a moment, she pulled the object out.

It was a familiar book. She read the cover, "Curses and Maledictions."

"You should keep that book and remember that setbacks are not failures. Keep trying, and you'll succeed," Teresa told her. "Besides, you never know what else you can learn from that book... About removing curses."

"Thank you," Laura said. She looked through the book again.

Teresa sat back down.

It was Walter's turn to talk. "Scotty, what about you? What stood out to you?"

"I loved the castle," Scotty said. "I liked the moat and the gate with the portcullis, and it would drop, and there were murder holes above so the defenders could stop the invaders from entering the castle. And the dungeon with the secret door and room. And the..."

Walter interrupted him. "So pretty much all the castle."

Scotty blushed. "Pretty much," he said.

Walter picked up a box from the table and handed it to his son.

Scotty instantly pulled the lid from the box. After just a glance inside, he grabbed a book from the box and dropped the box on the floor.

"Castle Construction," he read. "'How to build castles from the Ground Up.' Awesome!"

He started paging through the book right away.

Walter sat back down and watched his son page through the book with a smile.

It was Edna's turn to talk. "What about you, Sadie?" she asked.

Sadie thought about it for a while. "I guess the best thing about this trip was meeting our relatives and learning a little history of the MacGregors."

"And that's important to you?"

"I didn't think about it much before," she said. "But after seeing the castle and knowing that our family has lived there for centuries, I realized I didn't know as much about our family as I thought."

Edna picked up one of the remaining boxes and handed it to her daughter.

Inside the box, she found another book. "A History of Clan MacGregor," she read. "It's a history of our family?"

"Yes," Edna said. "Maeve said that they had several copies made, and she gave one to us. You can have it."

Sadie opened it up and quickly paged to the end of the book. She read several of the last pages.

"We're in here!" she said, reading aloud about Walter, Edna, and their two children, Sadie and Scott.

"She said that they update the original book whenever someone new is born into the family," Edna told her.

Sadie closed the book. "Thank you," she said.

Edna returned to her seat.

C.J. looked at his dad. "Is that mine?" he asked, pointing to the last box on the table.

"In a moment," Angus told him. "First, tell us what on this trip meant the most to you?"

"It's the same as on all our trips," he said. "I love discovering new things about the world."

"New things, like what?" Angus asked.

"We've never been to Scotland before. It was fun to learn about life here and how it differs from our life back home. And even though it was dangerous, I loved learning about curses and that a curse could create a thing like the knight."

"That's what I thought," his father said as he picked up the last box from the table.

When he accepted the box from his dad, C.J. almost thought he felt it move. He pulled the lid off and looked inside.

He almost threw the box across the room. "Why would I want this?" he said. At the bottom of the box was the knight's gauntlet. The fingers of the hand were slowly moving. Next to it was a piece of paper.

His father laughed. "The gauntlet is not actually for you. But the note is."

C.J. fished the note out of the box, avoiding the grasping fingers. His father took the box back and replaced the lid.

"Gauntlet from the Cursed Scottish Knight," he read. "Donated to the museum by Cameron Jules Kask."

He looked up at his father. "It will have my name on it?"

"Maeve said it should go to a museum, but she didn't want credit for it. Since you fought with it, she thought you could take the credit."

C.J. looked down at the note and smiled.

But then he frowned. "Could all four of us have our names on it? No, five. Keir's name should be on it too. We all fought the knight. We should all get credit."

"If that's what you want," Angus said.

"I do," C.J. said. "We're a team. We're the Young Explorers."

Don't miss out!

Visit the website below and you can sign up to receive emails whenever S T Cameron publishes a new book. There's no charge and no obligation.

https://books2read.com/r/B-A-CWRB-QONRG

BOOKS 2 READ

Connecting independent readers to independent writers.

Also by S T Cameron

The Young Explorers
Inca Wraith
Phantom Express
Scottish Knight

Watch for more at www.stcameron.com.

About the Author

I tell stories and have adventures.When I was a little boy, I would tell stories and have adventures in the backyard pretending I was in a circus in front of an audience of my family and neighbors. In elementary school, more stories and adventures were played out on the stage in front of my class and, sometimes, the entire school.In High School and College, I donned my glasses and disguised my super writer self in my computer nerd persona and while I still told stories and had adventures, they were never made publicly known.Many years later, I decided that it was time to remove my disguise and let my stories out in the world again.Outside of writing, I have adventures with Kay, my wife and future author of her own books, my two wonderful daughters and their families including four grand-children and two grand-puppies. I also let people know what is going on with my writing at stcameron.com.

Read more at www.stcameron.com.

www.ingramcontent.com/pod-product-compliance
Lightning Source LLC
Chambersburg PA
CBHW032023240626
47154CB00003B/764